LUCAS'S LADY

Sunset Valley Book 1

CAROLINE LEE

About the Book

Lucas Ryan has a problem.

The rustling and land-grabbing on his ranch has been going on far too long and he's been assured it'll stop just as soon as he married and produced an heir. So he's sent off for a mail-order bride who won't ask questions and wants a baby as much as he does.

There. *Problem solved.*

He just didn't count on falling in love with the woman.

Shannon Montgomery never thought she'd be a bride

She's spent her life being told she's undesirable,thanks to the large birthmark on her face. Becoming a mail-order bride to a man who had never seen her seemed the ideal answer, but she's eaten up with guilt for not confessing her imperfection to him ahead of time. Because in all her daydreaming about one day having children to dote on, she *definitely* didn't count on giving her heart to her husband quite so quickly!

And now they're out of luck.

Lucas's problem doesn't go away with his marriage; if anything, it gets worse. Now Shannon is in danger too, and the gunslinger Lucas hired to protect her is hiding terrible secrets of his own. Although Lucas is falling for his wife and becoming desperate to protect her, these revealed secrets call him to face his past and question everything he thought he knew. How can he give his heart when nothing is as it seems?

For my favorite Shannons.

Chapter One

The worn paper crinkled in her hands as Shannon unfolded the letters yet again. She smoothed them carefully against the blue of her skirt, a little afraid they might rip at the folds, but wanting to read his words again. Of course, she had both letters memorized by now, but there was just something special about seeing *his* hand-writing.

My dear Miss Montgomery,

From your description, you sound ideal. I've always been partial to blonde hair and blue eyes, and I can tell you're as beautiful inside as you are on the outside. Additionally, your eagerness to start a family will suit well with my goals, and I'm certain we will be well-matched. Once you reach the Montana Territory, you and I will be—

"You're going to rip those, if you read them too much more."

Shannon started in guilt, but resisted the urge to shove

the papers back into her reticle. Instead, she glanced at her sister, seated beside her. Cora had been staring out the window since the train's last stop, but now was looking down at Shannon with a faintly amused smile.

Cora always managed to make Shannon feel a little... well, *little*. Not only was she gorgeous, and significantly taller than Shannon, but Cora was well-traveled and well-educated, and had very clear plans for her life. Shannon's dreams always felt *little* beside her sister's. A husband. Children. Keeping a loving home. Small dreams. And maybe, *finally*, achievable ones.

"And if you rip them, you won't have anything to show your children when they ask how you met their daddy."

And somehow, despite their differences, Cora could make Shannon smile with only a few words. The older woman might not share the simple dream of a husband and children, but she never belittled Shannon for dreaming about it. Encouraged it, even.

"If I rip a letter," Shannon quipped, "then I'll save both halves. And I'll keep reading both of them."

Cora snorted. "You won't need to read them, silly. You'll have Mr. Ryan in *person* soon enough. He'll be able to tell you such romantic drivel every day—and night." She winked, a smile threatening her lips, and Shannon blushed.

She knew that, thanks to her painter friends, Cora was rather *Bohemian* in her approach to life—and love—but Shannon didn't mind. Sometimes it was nice to have an older sister who could explain certain things. Like how, exactly, Shannon should go about achieving her dream of —*ahem*—having babies. Still, imagining actually *doing* those certain things was another story altogether. Especially doing them with a man she'd never met, and barely knew.

"I hardly think—"

Cora hurried to continue. "Of course, if everything goes the way we planned, Mr. Ryan won't be spilling romantic drivel at night at all. He'll be too busy with *other* concerns." Her second wink was much more exaggerated, and she nudged Shannon with an elbow.

Shannon tried to roll her eyes at her sister's outrageous teasing, but knew she'd blushed when Cora began to laugh outright.

Thanks to the ugly red birthmark which covered her left cheek and traveled up past her temple into her hairline, Shannon hated to blush. She was afraid it made her look like an apple, but unfortunately, the littlest innuendo from Cora—especially if it concerned matters of the opposite sex—could cause her to glow embarrassingly.

So when her sister continued to laugh, Shannon managed a convincing frown in her direction. "You promised you wouldn't embarrass me in front of Mr. Ryan."

"He's not here, is he?" Cora nudged her again. "Besides, a little teasing about sex isn't going to kill you."

Oh Heavens! She'd said the *S-word*. "Cora, not everyone is as promiscuous—"

"*Enlightened*, thank you very much."

Shannon sighed, giving up. "Please just don't say such things in front of Mr. Ryan."

"Why? If you want the children you've been talking about forever, you're going to have to talk about all *sorts* of things with him, right? And perhaps, even manage to *do* some of those things."

Swallowing, Shannon focused on carefully folding the letters once more to tuck them into her bag. "I know," she said quietly. She *did* know. And truthfully, part of her was looking forward to becoming Mr. Ryan's wife, in every way. He'd described himself as strong and successful, and she

3

knew he was educated and polite from his letters. What woman *wouldn't* find that attractive in a man?

One thing was for sure, Shannon was not picky about appearances. Mr. Ryan hadn't told her anything about how he looked, and frankly, he could be ugly as sin, and Shannon wouldn't say boo. After all, it wasn't as if she'd been particularly truthful in her letters. She'd told him she was a blonde, yes, and petite...but never once had she mentioned the hideous birthmark on her face. The one which made it impossible to find a husband back in Texas.

And the whole reason she'd become a mail-order bride in the first place.

So no, she didn't honestly care what Mr. Ryan looked like. He sounded like a good man in his letters, and that was good enough for her. She'd marry him and keep his house and have his babies.

Assuming he didn't take one look at her and put her back on the train.

"Uh-oh." Cora's hand found hers. "You're worrying again, aren't you?"

Shannon nodded. She'd confessed her lie-by-omission to her sister on the day they'd left for Montana, but Cora hadn't thought it a big deal. And, judging from the way she squeezed her hand now, still didn't.

"Sweetheart, he won't care. I promise. He'll love you because you're good and kind and sweet and ridiculously eager to please."

Shannon's lips curled slightly at her sister's joking compliment. "You think?"

"I *know*." Cora sighed. "But I *also* know you're not going to accept my word for it."

"We're supposed to be married in town. When we arrive, I mean. Today." Shannon was whispering, but couldn't help it. She was just so *nervous*.

4

Cora squeezed her hand once more. "And you will be. And then tonight…"

Tonight, she'd officially become Mrs. Lucas Ryan.

Shannon swallowed. "What if he takes one look at me and decides I'm not worthy of him? What if he sends me —*us*—back home? I don't want to live with Joshua anymore. I want my own house, my own family."

Oh dear, she'd sounded quite pitiful there, hadn't she?

But Cora merely smiled kindly. "Sweetie, you have to trust me. I've read Mr. Ryan's letters too, remember? He's a good man. A man who won't judge a person based on appearance. And he'll value you for what he's read about *you* too, you know."

Shannon prayed her sister was right. Maybe the fact she'd lied to her husband-to-be wouldn't matter once they were married and settled. Maybe he truly *would* learn to look past her face, to her heart. And maybe, *maybe*, he'd learn to love her, just a bit.

Cora untangled her fingers from Shannon's, then pressed them against the window of the train. "Are you excited to be living up here?"

It was an obvious attempt at changing the subject, but Shannon latched onto it gratefully. "I don't think I care *where* I live, as long as it isn't with our brothers. As long as I have my own home."

"I don't need my own home," Cora murmured, staring now at the distant mountains. "I like being free. But this land…!" She took a deep breath, then pressed her forehead to the glass. "I can't wait to try to capture it. It's gorgeous."

Cora was a talented painter and was lucky to have made some money on her travels to New York and Paris. She could afford to travel and paint as much as she wanted, and part of Shannon envied her. Didn't envy the fact that she didn't want a home, no… But maybe envied how easily her sister was able to achieve her dreams, while Shannon herself had been waiting for so long.

But she just swallowed. "I can't wait to see your version."

"I doubt I'll be able to grasp it all on the first try, but I look forward to the attempt."

Shannon doubted her older sister was even listening anymore, she was so focused on the landscape whizzing by. "It'll be beautiful."

"Blue" Cora muttered. "Blues and greens, I think. Pinks in the clouds, maybe?"

No, her sister had slipped into her own little world of paint hues and ratios. Shannon had appreciated having someone to chat with and take her mind off her worries, but it was probably for the best she'd lost her sister's attention. She should use the time to prepare herself to meet her husband.

And to pray.

Pray he was as good a man as his letters made him sound, and he would be able to look past her face and into her heart.

Soon. So she could start the family she'd been dreaming about.

———

LUCAS PACED the tiny train platform outside of Black Aces, waiting for his bride to arrive and ignoring the occasional jokes Blake and Sam threw his way. The foreman and ranch hand had claimed they needed to come to town today, and had offered to help drive the buckboard and load up the future Mrs. Ryan's trunks. But judging from the fact they were now lounging against the wagon and teasing him about "finally" having a woman, he suspected they were just here to collect fodder for later.

The problem with trying to run the ranch where you'd grown up was that, well, everyone knew you when you were growing up. Lucas had inherited his father's spread four years ago and had worked hard to show the men he'd learned his father's lessons and could handle Sunset Valley Ranch on his own. And for the most part, they respected him, he thought. But that didn't mean they couldn't tease him about stupid stuff.

Like the fact he was getting married today.

Married. His mother had been after him to marry since his father's death, and it seemed wrong to be taking that step without her.

Unconsciously, Lucas's fingers dipped into his pocket where he'd taken to carrying around his mother's chain. She'd worn it for most of his life, and he'd gotten used to seeing the locket swinging beside her wedding ring and key around her neck. She'd begun wearing the ring on a chain because her fingers had swelled after his birth, and the locket was engraved with his initials. The key was to her lockbox at the bank, as far as he knew.

A train whistle, far off in the distance, jerked him from his musings, and he whipped his head around to peer eastward. She was coming.

He'd sent Miss Shannon Montgomery a train ticket himself, so he knew exactly when she was supposed to arrive. All he had to do was look for a petite blonde woman, traveling with her older sister, and he'd have his future wife.

Although he'd told himself it wouldn't matter what she looked like, part of him was secretly glad his bride was a blonde—he'd always been partial to the hair shade. Unfortunately, there weren't any blonde women—or *any* woman

—available to marry in these parts. And although Lucas was only twenty-two, he very much needed to get married.

So he'd sent away for a bride, and had appreciated the things Miss Montgomery had told him about herself. She was accomplished, and polite, and well-reared. She'd not only do well as his wife, but as the mistress of a successful cattle ranch.

Or rather, a cattle ranch which *would* be successful, just as soon as its future was assured by Lucas's marriage. Lucas's marriage and subsequent heir-begetting, at least.

The train whistle blew again, closer this time, and he swallowed. He was getting married, and if everything went well, the heir-begetting would happen that very night. And then, according to his mother's reasoning at least, Sunset Valley's future would be secure, and the rustling would cease.

"You're making me dizzy," Matthias Blake called out from where he lounged by the wagon. "Calm down. She'll be here soon enough."

Lucas paused to shoot his foreman a scowl, but the older man just chuckled.

Sam jabbed Blake in the side with his elbow. "He's probably worried about the beddin' mor'n' the weddin'!" he chortled.

Blake smiled and met Lucas' eyes with the agreement to drop the subject. "I think it'll be alright," he said quietly. Surely.

Lucas needed that surety. He sank down on the back of the wagon bed with a sigh, grateful for his friend's support. "Did you get those supplies we needed from Gomez's mercantile?"

Blake crossed one booted foot in front of the other and crossed his thick arms in front of his chest. "Yessir. Although prices have gone up since Mr. King waltzed his way into town demanding rent. But we'll make it through, no problem."

The other man was probably Lucas' closest friend, even though he was technically Blake's employer. Blake had been the one to help him navigate owning the ranch, and had never once indicated he thought Lucas was too young or too inexperienced. They still had a ways to go, but Lucas was glad for the man's support.

Staring at the not-so-distant column of smoke which marked the train—and his bride's—arrival, Lucas swallowed heavily. "You ever been married, Matthias?"

Blake shook his head sharply. "Never. Haven't seen a lot of use for it either, in all my thirty-three years. But maybe now you're getting married, some things'll change around the ranch…"

Lucas shrugged, not sure he was ready to admit how badly he wanted things to change. He *needed* things to change, and not just because he was lonely. When he was married and had a babe on the way, the rustling and threats to the ranch would cease.

Hopefully.

All too short a time later, Lucas stood, shifting his weight from foot to foot while the few passengers disembarked. Black Aces wasn't a big enough stop for anyone to get off and stretch their legs, so the only people climbing down from the train were—

There!

A petite blonde woman and a taller brunette. That had to be Miss Montgomery and her sister, Cora! Lucas strode toward them as the porter handed down their trunks. Sam and Blake jumped forward to help—about time they did something useful—but Lucas had eyes only for his bride.

And when her eyes met his for the first time, he halted, and she blushed slightly and turned away. Not so far he couldn't see her, but she turned her face just enough so he couldn't see most of her expression. The tall woman said something to her, but Miss Montgomery shook her head once, a look of panic on the half of her face he *could* see.

Her worry—what was she worried about?—hit Lucas like a punch to the sternum, and he suddenly very much wanted to make things better. He was moving toward the women again before he was even aware of it. All he could think of was the need to make her feel better.

Unfortunately, he reached the pair without any clear idea of *how* to make her feel better. Or even what was wrong. But once he stood in front of her, he couldn't *not* try.

So Lucas yanked off his hat and reached for her hand. Maybe it was forward. Maybe it was presumptuous, but he did it.

He reached for her hand, and his world changed.

Because the moment the callused skin of his fingers touched her smooth, delicate palm, a warmth shot up his arm, and he knew. Knew that, somehow, he'd found his match.

That warmth traveled through his chest and he told himself he was only aroused because he knew what was coming that night, but it was a lie. *This* woman, whom he hadn't even met yet, aroused him.

And judging from the way her lovely sky-blue eye—the one he could see—widened slightly, then flickered downward, she felt it too. A lazy, confident grin crept across Lucas's face.

Oh yeah, this was the woman for him.

"Miss Montgomery?"

"Yes."

He hadn't needed the confirmation, but her choked whisper was welcome.

"I'm Lucas Ryan. Welcome to Montana Territory."

"Thank you, Mr. Ryan."

She shifted slightly, as if to include her sister in the conversation, but Lucas wasn't ready to invite others into their private moment just yet. So he squeezed her hand, and her gaze flew to his.

Her whole gaze. She'd turned to him, and he saw her whole face. She really was lovely, wasn't she? Her blonde hair had been pulled back under her bonnet, but wisps escaped to frame her heart-shaped face in such a way that made Lucas's fingers itch to smooth them back. She had a pert little nose, wide eyes under delicate arches of her eyebrows, and plump lips which were currently parted slightly in surprise.

It wasn't until she glanced down, fixing her gaze squarely on his chin, that Lucas saw the large red birthmark on her left cheek. When she blushed, it was hardly noticeable, but reminded him of the strawberry mark he had on his arm, and the way it blended in when he'd been in the sun too long.

He wondered if that's what she'd been hiding when she stepped off the train.

Mentally, Lucas shrugged. He had a lifetime to prove she didn't have to hide from him. The way his body had reacted—was *still* reacting—to her said she was gorgeous just the way she was. He couldn't wait to get to know her; to see if she was as beautiful inside as out.

This time, when he squeezed her hand, he pulled slightly too, so that her gaze snapped back up to his at the same time she was forced to take a step closer. He inhaled deeply, appreciating her faint floral scent in the May air.

Could she feel the warmth between them? Is that why her skin was so flushed? Why she swallowed suddenly—he couldn't help studying the skin not-quite-hidden by her lace collar—or why the pulse in her wrist hammered so frantically?

Lucas's grin grew. He sure hoped so.

"I'd hoped

you'd call me Lucas, Miss Montgomery. Since we'll be married soon."

Her nod was hesitant, but she didn't drop his gaze. This time, when she swallowed, her tongue darted out to moisten her lower lip, and Lucas's breath caught. Did she know how enticing she was?

"Lucas." She inclined her head slightly, her voice hesitant. "And you should call me Shannon."

"And you can call me Cora." The taller woman didn't bother to hold out her hand, but placed hers on her hips—

Was that a man's shirt she was wearing? It was too big, too flowing on her, for certain. And she wore the reform bloomers, which had gone out of style decades ago, tucked into tall boots, as if she were about to climb on a horse or a bicycle. With her brown hair lying in a girlish braid over one shoulder, and her smile a bit too wide, she was a study in contradiction. Lucas supposed Cora Montgomery might've been considered handsome, but as he compared her to her sister, he was quite pleased he was contracted to marry the *pretty* Montgomery daughter.

But he didn't let his thoughts show. Instead, he brushed his thumb along the inside of Shannon's palm and nodded respectfully to her sister. "Miss Cora, welcome to Montana. I hope the journey was pleasant."

His soon-to-be sister in law waved dismissively, then turned to the mountains, inhaling deeply. "Train travel has come a long way in the last decade, I'll agree. I'm glad to be here." Her gaze—the same shade as Shannon's—flicked over their clasped hands, and she smiled. "Thank you for allowing me to visit."

In one of Shannon's letters, she'd requested permission for her sister to live with them for an undisclosed amount of time. Lucas couldn't see the harm in the request, since there were so few marriageable women in the area. Of course, now that he'd met Cora Montgomery, he couldn't imagine who'd want to marry her, but she was welcome to stay in the ranch's guest room as long as she wanted.

So he just nodded and smiled in return, before turning back to his bride. Shannon was gazing down at where his thumb was making lazy circles against her skin, looking a little shocked.

At the warmth between their skin? At the instant connection they'd shared? Or did she not feel it at all?

That connection had set Lucas at ease, but maybe it made her uncomfortable. Whatever it was, it meant he was a heck of a lot less nervous now than he'd been before the train rumbled into the station.

So he smiled confidently and lifted her hand to his lips. Her eyes widened at the gesture, but she didn't look away. "My dear Shannon, Reverend Trapper is waiting for us at the church. Would you like me to find you someplace to freshen up before the wedding?"

He'd expected a blushing agreement, and perhaps some thanks for his manners. But instead, she took a deep breath—he managed not to peer at her blouse when she did so—and lifted her chin.

"If it's all the same to you, Mr. Ry—*Lucas*, I would prefer to marry you quickly and see my new home. Presumably I can freshen up there?"

His grin grew. Oh yes, she'd do well as mistress of his family's ranch. "I like the sound of that."

The train blew its whistle and began to pull away from the station, but the Montgomery sisters' trunks were already loaded into the wagon. Cora and Blake stood ready to act as witnesses to the ceremony, so there was no reason to delay.

Lucas jammed his hat back on his head, offered Shannon his arm, and asked "Shall we, Miss Montgomery?"

Her movements were hesitant when she snaked her hand through his offered arm, but he saw her inhale deeply right before she met his eyes. "Yes please, Mr. Ryan."

"Alright then," he whispered. They'd head for the church…just as soon as he could tear his gaze away from her gorgeous sky-blue eyes. "Let's go get married."

Chapter Two

S hannon released a deep sigh when Lucas rolled off her. That had been *incredible*!

His arm was still around her shoulders, so she shifted slightly to find a more comfortable position, then allowed herself to slowly unclench the muscles in her legs. Who knew making love would be so...so athletic? The soles of her feet had flexed so hard, she wasn't sure she'd be able to walk anytime soon.

Not that she felt like walking now, that is. Not with her *husband* pressed up against her, all warm and slick with sweat.

Mrs. Lucas Ryan. She was married now. Well and truly married, thanks to what they just did. She was a wife, and if they kept this up, she'd be a mother soon enough.

That thought didn't distract her the way it normally would've. No, she was too busy focusing on the wonder of being a *wife*. Cora had hinted that making love would feel nice, assuming it was done properly, but this—?

Nice didn't begin to cover it.

There'd been some pain, yes, but not nearly as much as

she'd dreaded, especially after he'd made her feel so good. Who knew a tongue could be so useful? Certainly not Shannon, in all of her years of imagining and daydreaming.

Lucas shifted beside her, his arm tightening around her, until she was pressed full-length against him. In the darkness it was only a little embarrassing, but she still hesitated before inching her cheek to his shoulder. They were newlyweds. Surely it was still too early to show such affection?

But then, she'd been ready to show him affection within moments of meeting him. She'd met his eyes across the station platform and had just *known* he was the man for her. He was tall—not overly, but just enough she'd had to look up into his eyes—and handsome, although his features were unremarkable on their own merits. Light brown hair with a touch of curl, golden-brown eyes, a firm jaw and a wide mouth, and his features came together to form the man of her dreams.

Up until that moment, Shannon had thought her dream of becoming a mother would forever be the strongest she'd know. She hadn't spared a moment's thought for the *father* of those hypothetical children...but when he'd taken her hand in his, and began to trace little circles on her skin with his callused thumb, she'd suddenly been able to think about little else.

This was the man who'd father her children, and in that moment, she very, *very* much wanted to get started.

Lucas had made her *warm* all over, and his touch was special. What they'd just shared had proved it. Even as his breathing deepened and she lay her free palm gently on his chest to feel his heartbeat, Shannon knew the truth.

She'd made the right decision.

Her only hesitation was the way he'd stared at her birthmark. Oh, she was used to that; the stares and whispers had followed her her whole life. But Lucas hadn't said anything about it. In fact, he hadn't stared at it for too long either, which was a surprise. She had expected him to at least mention it, or ask her why *she* hadn't mentioned it.

Or rail against her for lying to him in her letters.

Or accuse her of being hideous and hand her a ticket for the next train back to Texas.

But instead, he'd just smiled at her, as if he didn't notice it at all, and that's what was bothering Shannon now, curled up beside him in the darkness.

How could he *not* notice it? It's all anyone saw when they looked at her—all *she* saw when she looked in the mirror. He *had* to have noticed it, but was just too polite to say anything.

Or…

Or was just biding his time. Maybe Mr. Lucas Ryan would still take drastic action against her for lying to him. She'd married him, yes, but she didn't *really* know anything about him. They'd shared something beautiful, but from Cora's stories, Shannon knew men didn't always need to engage their hearts when they engaged their bodies.

She'd always taken that to mean men could make love without *being* in love, and that was as it should be, right? After all, Lucas had just met *her* that day too. It would be silly to bemoan the fact they weren't in love yet, when they barely knew one another.

And silly to think she knew him well enough to be absolutely sure of his reaction to her lies.

She sighed again, taking wicked delight in the utterly foreign feel of a man's skin under her cheek. Love hadn't been a requirement for this marriage, and plenty of marriages began this way. Her mother had always told her children that if they were lucky, they'd make sound matches, which would grow into love. But that sort of growth required trust, and what Shannon had done—omitting such a flaw—had to hurt whatever chance she'd had of gaining her new husband's trust.

And his love.

"You're thinking awfully hard over there."

She jerked in surprise when Lucas spoke, and felt him chuckle beneath her hand.

"Sorry," he said, although he didn't sound sorry. In fact, he sounded as if he was smiling.

The realization made her defensive. "I thought you were asleep!"

Shannon moved to pull her hand off his chest, but he captured it and began rubbing those intoxicating circles on her palm again.

"And I figured *you'd* be asleep. After all, you should be exhausted. Days on a train, then you hop off and marry some stranger, who whisks you back to his house for debauchery."

Thank goodness it was dark, so he wouldn't see her blushing like a tomato. "Well, first he took me and my sister to dinner at a very nice restaurant."

"Ah, yes," Lucas said solemnly, still holding his hand in hers. "That should count for something."

"Yes." She cleared her throat, deciding maybe she didn't mind this holding-and-talking too much. Were they cuddling? Is that what they were doing? "I thought it very gentlemanly."

"It *was*, especially considering how badly your new husband wanted to skip ahead to the debauching."

He pulled her closer to him with that comment, and she couldn't help giggling at his suggestive tone. The darkness and the intimacy of what they'd just shared somehow freeing.

"I'll confess I might have been looking forward to that part a little as well."

At her whispered confession, she felt him tense beneath her, and his fingers stilled their caress. "Really?"

She wondered if she'd said the wrong thing. "Is that so...unusual?"

"I…" He took a breath deep enough to shift her cheek against his skin. "I don't know. I've never been married. But I assumed…" He trailed off, but his thumb resumed its caress. After a minute of silence, the palm of his other hand stroked down her backside, sending thoroughly wicked shivers through her. "You really were looking forward to this?"

How to answer? How to confess she'd felt the connection between them immediately, and that his touch had sent warmth through her belly and lower, even at their first meeting?

Instead, she took the careful path. "I told you in my letters I wanted children."

"Yes, you mentioned that was your dream."

"It was. I mean, it is," she quickly corrected. "I want children more than anything else."

"Why?" Maybe he felt her stiffen at his question, because he tightened his hold on her. "I mean, I know most women want children, but why would you want them more than anything else?"

Shannon wasn't sure how much to tell him. "Children love you unconditionally." They didn't care what their mother looked like; they'd love her because of who she was.

"That's true," he agreed, sounding pensive. "I loved my mother very much."

She knew from his letters that his mother had recently died. "I'm sorry you lost her."

"I am too. She was the one who pushed me to marry, so I wish she were still here to meet you."

"Really? You're only—" She bit down on her words, not sure if she might insult him.

But he chuckled. "Twenty-two. I was hoping for a few more years running wild, I'll admit."

The darkness made it easier for her to ask, "Then why marry?"

"Well…" His palm skimmed her backside once more. "The perks are nice."

Something about his flippant answer seemed false, and Shannon felt as if he was closing himself off against her. She stifled her sigh, knowing she'd done the very same to him, and rolled away, pulling her hand out of his as she went.

It made sense he'd keep secrets from her. After all, she'd kept a secret from him, and it was a big one. What did his reasoning for marrying matter?

But for some reason, deep down, Shannon knew it *did* matter. It mattered, not just to her, but to their future together.

———

"Hard day?"

Shannon's question jerked Lucas's attention to her, where she was sitting across the dinner table from him. "Huh?" he asked, then winced.

Not real articulate, are you?

"You haven't said much. I hope the food is alright?"

When he realized his wife—of two weeks!—was actually nervous about something, Lucas could've kicked himself. He should've made more of an effort to be charming and engaging. He hated to think she was still acting reserved around him.

"No! I mean, yes, the food's great." He took a big bite of the bread to prove his point. "This is delicious," he said around the mouthful, all the while knowing his mother would roll over in her grave to see him with such poor manners. "I love fresh bread."

Shannon blushed slightly, but didn't appear as if he'd convinced her. Her sister, however, interrupted his awkward attempts to reassure his wife.

"See?" She lifted an eyebrow and pointed at Shannon with a fork. "I told you he'd like it." When her sister merely ducked her head, Cora turned to Lucas, who was still chewing like a dolt. "Shannon makes the best bread, but won't admit it. Me? I'm all thumbs in the kitchen, but I can clean, at least. By the way, I moved that ugly vase out to the hall table." Before Lucas could process what she was saying, Cora smiled widely at her sister. "And Shannon is nice enough to let me help cook sometimes."

Shannon snorted slightly and finally raised her hand to pick up her fork. "If I don't give you a job, you take it upon yourself to 'help', and the results are disastrous."

She didn't look at her sister as she teased, but Lucas thought he could see a hint of a smile on his wife's lovely face.

"Sugar and salt look *exactly* the same. If you can't be bothered to label things properly, I can't be responsible for an honest mistake."

This time, Lucas was sure Shannon was smiling at her sister's banter, although she kept her attention on the chicken and gravy in front of her. "Anyone with a grain of sense would know to taste them if they're unlabeled."

"Really? How do I know it's not arsenic?"

Now Shannon met her sister's eyes, one beautifully

sculpted brow raised speculatively. "*Arsenic?* Why would I keep arsenic in my kitchen?"

"To poison me when I start tasting things, obviously."

The two sisters held each other's gazes for a long moment, before dissolving into giggles. It made Lucas's heart lighter to hear them, and he took another bite of his wife's dinner. He hadn't lied; it was good.

But he'd been distracted since he sat down, and knew it. He'd been vaguely aware of the two women bantering back and forth a bit as he'd stared down at his food, thinking about what he'd learned that day. But then they'd lapsed into silence, and he winced again to realize it had probably been due to the fact he hadn't participated.

He'd been married two weeks now, and dinners between the three of them were common. Much more fun than the solitary meals he'd eaten since his mother died, or the quiet meals he'd shared with the men in the bunk house. Occasionally, he and Blake had gone into Black Aces for meals, but they'd been nowhere near as delicious as Shannon's. She hadn't lied in her letters when she'd told him she could cook.

Meanwhile, Cora's offerings to the meals had been barely palatable, and he admired that she could admit it. The few paintings of hers he'd seen had convinced him this new sister-in-law of his should stick with her art and stay out of the kitchen as much as possible. He'd been surprised when Shannon had asked if her sister could stay with them, but was pleased now. Cora brought laughter to Sunset Valley and had saved things from being too awkward between Lucas and Shannon.

And things *were* awkward, much to his chagrin. Sure, that was probably to be expected, what with the whole "mail-order bride" thing. But…he'd had high hopes after feeling the attraction between them. After knowing how well they fit together.

Unfortunately, after that first day, Lucas was beginning to suspect they only "fit" together in bed. Their nights since their wedding had been…well, she'd been pretty much everything Lucas could've hoped for in a bed partner. That spark he'd felt between the two of them at the train station had caught, and he was pretty confident he'd have his heir by springtime.

The only problem was that as uninhibited and loving as Shannon was in bed with him, she was the complete opposite during the day. Granted, he was out working with the men most of the day, but when he'd see her in the mornings, or at dinner, she was shy. Almost nervous. He'd catch her looking at him as if she didn't know what to make of him, or as if she was waiting for him to do something she wouldn't like.

It didn't sit right with him, but he didn't know what to do about it. Didn't know how to convince his wife to open up to him and discuss her concerns. That's what husbands and wives were supposed to do, wasn't it?

"Lucas?"

Oh shoot, his thoughts had wandered off again. He wasn't sure what the women had been talking about after the laughter had ended, but he'd missed it. "Sorry. What?"

He caught the hesitant look Shannon sent to her sister. Cora made a little shooing motion, but then pretended a lot of interest in her almost-empty plate when she saw him looking. His eyes flicked back to his wife, and he raised a brow in question.

Despite his curiosity, he couldn't help but admire the way her body moved when she took a deep breath and straightened. He'd been appreciating that body an awful lot, but was at a loss for how to talk her into letting him appreciate her heart and mind too.

"I just asked if everything was okay?" She kept her gaze on him, but he saw her picking at the tablecloth. She was still nervous?

He sighed. "Yeah, everything's fine."

"You rode out today with Mr. Blake I noticed."

She'd noticed? He wasn't sure if he should take that for a good sign or not. Did she worry about him, the way a proper wife would?

"He had something he figured I should see."

His mood darkened when he thought about the almost-hidden traces of campsites and fires his foreman had shown him. Someone was out there, on his property, sticking close enough to the house to keep an eye on all of them. And Lucas had a pretty good idea who it was.

"What was it?"

His first instinct was to explain it to her. How many evenings had he and Mother sat across from one another, discussing ranch issues? She'd helped him talk through the problems until he understood the best solution. But she'd been a rancher's wife for far longer than Shannon had, and had understood all of the dangers and troubles.

Shannon was not only new to the cattle-ranching world, but new to Montana. She was still getting used to taking over a new household—apparently Mother hadn't bothered to label the salt and the sugar?—and a new husband. She was nervous enough around him and didn't need anything else to worry about.

So he just smiled as convincingly as possible, and said, "Nothing much. Nothing to worry about."

When her face fell, he knew he'd said something wrong.

The rest of the meal was quiet and awkward. Lucas

watched his wife from behind lowered lashes. She didn't take another bite after he'd upset her. Of course, he still didn't know *how* he'd upset her, but knew it was his fault, somehow.

Cora tried her best to keep conversation going, but even she eventually gave up. She helped clear the table, then excused herself to her room, as she did most nights. Lucas did catch her sending her sister a good glare before she left, and he wondered about it. Did Cora know what was bothering Shannon?

Maybe he should go after her, ask her to explain what he'd done wrong, and how to make it right. At the same time, Lucas was surprised his wife's good graces mattered so much to him. He didn't remember his father ever discussing issues with Mother, or worrying about his wife's opinion of him. But for some reason, Lucas did. Maybe it was his mother's influence, after all.

His musings were interrupted—yet again—by Shannon. She plucked the empty plate out of his hand, and turned to dunk it into the wash basin.

When had he joined her in the kitchen?

He grimaced. Between this worry of the unknown observer and his wife's poor opinion, he was getting too damn distracted.

He watched her elbows saw in and out as she scrubbed at the plate, and he sighed again. Her opinion *did* matter to him, and not just because he enjoyed her company in bed. He wanted to enjoy her company—and have her enjoy *his* company—out of bed too.

Still, he figured he could use their attraction to his advantage. He crossed the kitchen and slipped his arms around her waist.

She stiffened but didn't push him away. He took that to be a good sign. After a few heartbeats, he experimented with pulling her closer, and she seemed to close the gap between them willingly.

With her backside pressed against him like that, his breath stirred the tendrils of hair at the base of her neck that had escaped her bun. He loved her hair, loved to comb it through his fingers after they made love, but before she fell asleep. Now though, he had to keep himself from nuzzling her skin. Instead, he clasped his hands in front of her and tried to remember to *talk* to her.

"Dinner was delicious." There. Compliments were a good way to start.

Unfortunately, she didn't say anything in return. So he dropped a kiss to her ear. "I'm sorry I was so distracted, honey. Blake and I had—"

No. He didn't want to burden her with his worries.

He kissed her ear again, then the skin right below it where he knew she was particularly sensitive. "I should leave my work outside though, when I come home. Just focus on you."

Another kiss, and she still didn't respond. What else did she want to hear?

"I promise—"

He hadn't been sure what he'd been about to say, just that he was willing to promise a hell of a lot to get her to open up to him. But she interrupted him.

"Lucas?"

"Yeah, honey?" Another kiss, and when she moaned slightly and relaxed against him, he felt a surge of hope. "Why don't you talk to me?" he prompted.

She made a sexy little noise and tilted her head to one side, giving him better access. "About what?"

Hell if he knew. He just trailed kisses down her neck and murmured in between: "About your day. About what you were thinking about." *About why you haven't talked —really talked—to me since you married me.*

"Are you sure?"

He almost missed her whispered question, and it made him pause. "Yeah. Why wouldn't I be?"

"Because…" When she took a deep breath, he felt it throughout his whole body. "You don't seem that interested in *talking*." Her backside shifted slightly against the *very* interested part of him, and he knew what she meant.

Chagrined, he pulled back slightly, but didn't relax his hold on her. "You do that to me, honey."

She snorted. It didn't sound like a laugh, more like she didn't believe him. Or didn't approve of his claim.

"What? What do you want me to say?" Dammit, he hadn't meant for those words to come out so harsh, but he was frustrated. She was rebuffing all of his attempts.

"The truth."

The truth? "I am—"

"No." She turned in his arms, and despite the stiffness of her posture—was she trying to hold herself away from him?—she didn't look angry. Not the way Mother used to get sometimes when he didn't take her advice, at least. No, Shannon looked… exasperated? "You're telling me things you think I want to hear."

He clamped down on his first instinct to deny it, to tell her he was speaking the truth. But… she was right. He *was* trying to ingratiate himself by saying things he thought would make her happy.

He shifted his hands to her hips and narrowed his eyes as he tried to read her face. "What do you want me to say then?"

She was still holding the dish towel she'd used to dry her hands when he'd reached for her, but now she placed one hand on his arm. "Why did you marry me, Lucas?"

The question was surprising enough to make him rear back. "Because you answered my ad and sounded like a good match. I thought you agreed we were a good fit and —" He frowned, wondering if she was already regretting this marriage.

"No, I mean…" She patted his forearm slightly, as if trying to reassure him. Reassure *him*? "Why did you marry at all?"

When his brows dipped down in confusion, she glanced away, but continued. "I asked you that on our wedding night, if you remember. You…didn't respond."

He remembered. He'd given her a flippant answer then, and stopped himself from repeating the same mistake now, just before she continued.

"I'm still curious though. You're young and have a successful ranch. You mentioned you didn't expect to marry so soon, and you obviously have resources…" She met his eyes once more. "You didn't need to get married, but you did. Just because your mother told you to?"

There wasn't anything accusing in her words, but Lucas felt uncomfortable anyhow. As if he'd been caught in a lie. As if he were still a little boy.

His jaw hardened, and he pulled away from her.

"Lucas?"

The pleading tone in her voice tugged at something in his chest.

"Talk to me. Please."

He turned slightly, but couldn't bring himself to leave the room completely. "I married you the same reason you married me. Babies."

"You want a child?"

Now she sounded surprised. And why wouldn't she? It was a silly answer from such a young man, he knew.

"More than one, hopefully."

Silence from her, then from the corner of his eye he saw her toss down the dish towel. "You're still not being honest with me, are you?"

"What? Yes I am!" Lucas ran his hand through his hair as he stepped even farther away, not understanding what it was she wanted from him. "I told you I wanted kids, that's why I got married."

She stared at him for long enough he became uncomfortable, so he crossed to the counter where the second loaf of bread sat. He knew it was supposed to be for breakfast tomorrow, but he began to pick at the crust anyway.

"What?" Lucas muttered, irritated over how he could feel so petulant.

"I've sat across from you every evening at dinner for two weeks, Lucas. Breakfast too, but you don't talk as much then. You're well-spoken, and funny, and smart. You've let me see a lot of *you*, and I'm glad I've gotten to know you, but…"

He kept picking at the bread, waiting for her to continue.

Eventually she did. "You told me your mother pushed you to marry. Did she want grandchildren?"

Lucas snorted. "What kind of mother doesn't?" But he knew he had to tell her *something*. "But you're right, it was more than that." He took a breath. "I need an heir."

"You're awfully young to be worried about dying and passing your ranch on to someone, aren't you? My father was almost thirty when my oldest brother was born."

"No, I…" Damn, how to explain it? "If I have an heir, things will…be better."

He'd hoped his vagueness would satisfy her, and he wouldn't need to worry her any further. No such luck.

"What things?"

Lucas sighed. "My neighbor is causing some trouble,

but once I have an heir, I think he'll lay off." It had been what his mother had claimed, at least, and he'd thought it was a pretty convincing argument.

"Is he less likely to harass a man who has children?"

"He's less likely to try to take over Sunset Valley if he realizes he doesn't have claim to it anymore."

Aw, shoot. He hadn't meant to say so much, but it had just sort of slipped out. Was she going to worry now, knowing one of their neighbors was trying to run them off his own land?

But Shannon didn't say anything. He heard her moving around behind him and the sound of dinner dishes being put away. It was a good five minutes before he felt her warmth beside him, and he didn't have to even look up to know she was there.

She reached around him and pulled the bread he was destroying out of his reach, carefully tucking it into a towel and knotting it up so the loaf wouldn't get too hard overnight. He knew from the last two weeks she'd cut up the bread tomorrow and fry it in egg and milk and sugar, and he found himself looking forward to it already. When had she become such a huge part of his life? When had he come to value her so much?

Instead of walking away when she was finished with that simple task, she turned to face him and caught him staring at her rear end.

Whoops.

Lucas crossed his arms in front of his chest and leaned one hip against the counter, wondering if he could convince her to head upstairs so he could show her just how much he *appreciated* her.

But the look on her face convinced him to keep his mouth shut. She wasn't done talking about the whole needing-an-heir thing. He watched her open her mouth, then shut it again, and drop her eyes to her hands on the counter.

"Lucas, I…"

He sighed. *He'd* done that to her, made her feel so nervous. How? When he'd tried so hard to keep her from having anything to worry about. What could make her feel so uncomfortable around him?

He reached out and grabbed one of her hands, twining his fingers through hers. "I'm sorry, Shannon." He didn't know exactly what he was apologizing for, but he was sorry she didn't feel comfortable enough around him to talk to him.

His gesture must've given her strength, because she met his eyes once more. "I feel as if you're not telling me everything, Lucas. I'm your wife. Surely you can tell me who this man is, and why he's causing you—*us*—so much trouble?"

She wanted to know *more*?

With a swiftness that might've knocked his head back, Lucas realized the truth. Here he'd been, moping about how his wife wasn't sharing her thoughts and feelings with him, when *he* was the one who'd been keeping things from *her*. Sure, he'd done it because he cared about her and wanted to keep her from worrying, but was that a good enough reason? Maybe she was as disappointed in the way things had been going between them as he was!

So he moved toward the small desk in the corner where his mother had written out her recipes and the household accounts, tugging Shannon along by the hand. When he settled himself in the chair, he pulled her down too. Her startled squeak told him she hadn't expected to land on her husband's lap, but he only grinned.

Lifting his hand, he brushed the backs of his fingers down her left cheek. She flinched and turned away slightly, and he wondered if her birthmark was more sensitive or something for her to respond that way. Still, with her chin turned like that, he had a view of her gorgeous neck.

She really was lovely, wasn't she?

"My father wasn't a real nice man, and his old partner isn't either. My father and Pierce used to work all of this land together, but they split it into two separate ranches right after my parents' marriage. They'd agreed they'd each inherit the other's land if one of them died."

Shannon didn't say anything, but didn't have to; when she turned back to him slowly, he could read the interest in her eyes.

"And that seemed like it'd be fine, for the first years, but eventually I came along, and Dad raised me to take over his ranch. When he died, the trouble started."

"What kind of trouble?" Her arm snaked around his shoulders, and she began to rub the muscles at the base of his neck.

It felt all kinds of good, after the hours in the saddle that day, but Lucas resisted the urge to groan. He *did* tilt his head forward slightly, to give her better access.

"It was slow at first. Missing calves, ruined fences, cattle with indistinct brands. The sheriff in town is pretty useless, and the issues have gotten worse over the last few years, to the point where it's obvious Pierce is trying to ruin Sunset Valley. When I lose all my money, he'll buy up the property."

"You're sure it's your father's partner? This Mr. Pierce?"

Beyond a doubt. "Yeah. He's offered to buy me out at least eight times. I stopped counting, but every time we meet in town, he's bragging about how this land is supposed to be his, and how my father didn't have any right to leave it to me."

Her fingers stilled briefly, then resumed their kneading.

"But that's… You're your father's son. Of course the land should come to you."

Lucas snorted. "I know. And to my son or daughter after me." He tightened his hold on her waist and placed one hand on her stomach. "That's why I needed to get married. So I could be sure Pierce knew he wasn't getting the land." *No matter what happens to me.* "I need a son or daughter, as soon as possible."

He loved the way her cheeks pinked until they matched her birthmark, and how she bit her lower lip. Did she realize how enticing she was when she did that? Probably not.

"I want children as soon as possible too," she whispered.

"Well, alright then." Lucas began to stand, still holding her, but when she tightened her hold on him, he stopped.

"But I still don't understand why you believe having children would solve this, Lucas. Mr. Pierce's offers to purchase won't end just because you have an heir."

Oh, damn.

His wife was apparently smarter than he'd given her credit for, and Lucas *knew* she'd worry if she knew the whole truth. Yeah, Joseph Pierce wasn't going to stop trying to *buy* the Ryan land if Lucas had an heir, but purchasing the land wasn't all Pierce had tried.

There had been a number of mysterious accidents around the ranch over the last year, and Lucas had barely escaped unscathed from two of them. Hay bales didn't just fall out of the hayloft on their own, and his cinch strap had definitely been cut during the spring. Pierce was trying to have Lucas killed, so the ranch would revert back to him.

In fact, Pierce had even hired a gunslinger to ensure it happened.

Two-Grins Baker had been seen in town with Pierce

several times in the last months, and Lucas *knew* he was the one who had been camping on his land, watching. Waiting.

It was pretty damn terrifying to know one of the fastest guns-for-hire in the west was after his blood, but Lucas had sent a telegram the week before he'd married Shannon, and hoped he'd soon have his own protection. His own protector.

With a gunslinger by *his* side, and an heir in his wife's womb, Pierce would *have* to realize he'd never get the land. It would all go to Mrs. Lucas Ryan, and their son or daughter.

Whom Shannon might even now be carrying.

So he shifted his hold until his free arm was under her legs, then stood, holding her. Her squeal was even louder this time, and she wrapped both arms around his neck.

"What are you doing, Lucas?"

Distracting you.

"Ensuring we both get what we want, honey." He kissed her and was heartened by the way she melted against him. "After all, it's pretty hard to focus when you're sitting there looking so kissable." He trailed his lips across her left cheek to her ear. "So touchable," he whispered.

"Oh…" She was flustered, judging from her breathy reaction.

"After all, we both want babies. Better get started, Mrs. Ryan."

"Well, alright then," she smiled, parroting one of his favorite phrases. "Let's go make a baby, Mr. Ryan."

And they were both laughing as he carried her up the stairs.

This is what marriage should be.

Chapter Three

S hannon clutched her husband's arm in an effort to stay upright. She was nearly breathless from laughter, thanks to his quips about life in the small town of Black Aces. They were strolling along the boardwalk in front of the mercantile, and she almost pulled him to a stop so she could collapse on the benches placed out front.

"No! S*hhhh*!" He tugged on her hand in mock terror. "Don't stop here, honey," he whispered. "Mrs. Burch will see you and come out and insist on talking to you!"

She could tell from the twinkle in his eye he was still joking. "And would that be so horrible? I want to meet everyone in town, after all!"

"Better wait 'til winter—Christmas at least—to meet this particular townswoman." He tucked Shannon up against his side and hustled her along, their heads close enough together she didn't mind his teasing one bit. "The stench is less then, you see."

"Stench?" Shannon giggled. "She doesn't bathe?"

"Oh, no, she bathes regularly." Lucas finally deemed them out of danger and slowed his pace. Turning to her with a grin, he winked. "It's the onions, see. She chews one every morning to ward off bad humors."

Shannon dissolved into laughter once more. He'd kept her giggling throughout lunch at the town's only restaurant as well, and she couldn't recall enjoying herself this much in a very long time.

"But not in the winter?" she managed to ask, in between chuckles.

"Oh, she still does it in the winter." Lucas's expression was solemn when he nodded. "But then she chews a peppermint stick after, for seasonal variety."

Shannon blinked at her husband, thinking he couldn't possibly be serious, but he nodded and clarified. "She says peppermint and onion always remind her of Christmas."

That did it.

"That's disgusting!" Shannon began laughing so hard, she collapsed against Lucas, trusting him to support her. In fact, she was trusting him more and more, so it seemed.

They'd only been married three weeks, but she was happier here than when she'd been living with her brother Joshua and his wife back in Texas. Lucas Ryan made her feel *cherished*, which is more than she'd ever felt back home. Unlike her brothers' families, he didn't make her feel as if her appearance dictated her worth. He made her laugh and treated her like a goddess in bed. And after the conversation they'd had last week in the kitchen, when he'd told her about the dangers their neighbor Mr. Pierce posed, things were a lot more open between them.

She felt as if they were partners, now. For the last few dinners, the two of them and Cora had discussed ranch business, and she'd discovered her husband was an intelligent and educated man, with surprising insights into human nature. And he asked *her* opinion about all sorts of things, which made her feel valued in a way she never had before.

God help her, she was falling in love with her husband.

The thought was enough to sober her, and she straightened to tuck her hand in Lucas's arm once more. Her smile remained, though, as he began to lead her towards the bank once more.

She was falling in love with her husband, and what should have been a joyous realization just made her stomach hurt. He was kind and funny, and generous and thoughtful and even polite to her eccentric sister. Falling in love with him was easy!

But there were still things he was keeping from her. Things he wasn't telling her, and she suspected they had to do with some sort of danger at the ranch. Danger to *him*. Why would Mr. Pierce care about Lucas having an heir, unless he was threatening Lucas himself? But why wouldn't her husband explain these things to her?

There was only one explanation: he didn't trust her. He'd taken one look at her face, the face she'd lied about, and had decided if she could keep that sort of information from *him*, then he just wouldn't share everything with *her*.

And at night, when she was cuddled against him, listening to his faint and satisfied snores, she had to admit she couldn't blame him. How *could* he trust someone like her? Someone who'd manipulated a good, honest man into marriage by letting him think she was beautiful?

She was falling in love with her husband, but how could he ever love her in return?

Lucas didn't seem to realize the change in her emotions, and kept up his teasing until they turned into the bank. Shannon kept her smile plastered on, even when it became clear that Lucas was planning on introducing her to the banker.

"…and this is my wife. Shannon, this is Mr. Daniel Pearson."

"How do you do, sir?"

Perhaps Shannon's greeting would've been more enthusiastic—and from Lucas's glance, she knew that's what he'd been hoping for—but she'd seen the way Mr. Pearson eyed her cheek. Like most strangers, upon meeting her, the older gentleman did his best to hide the pity which had flashed into his expression, but it didn't matter. Shannon had seen it, and the way the banker couldn't seem to stop staring at it.

Soon, Mr. Pearson—and the lovely people she'd met at the restaurant, and maybe even Mrs. Burch—would begin to talk to one another about her. They'd ask how a successful rancher like Lucas had married someone as ugly as she, and then Shannon would have the guilt of ruining her husband's good name.

So she did her best to smile at Mr. Pearson, but knew her heart wasn't in it.

Lucas watched her with worry in his eyes. "I'm here for my mother's papers, Daniel." Without tearing his gaze away from her, Lucas fished something out of his pocket and held it towards the older man. "I'm pretty certain this key was the one she'd mentioned went to her box here."

"Looks like it."

Lucas finally glanced at the older man. "Any objection to me taking whatever she had stored in there? That's all legal, right?"

Shannon was relieved when the banker had turned his full attention to her husband, and began to breathe a little easier.

"Don't see why not." Mr. Pearson turned the key over in his hands. "She used to wear it on a chain around her neck, as I recall."

Lucas nodded. "Along with a locket and her ring." His free hand reached over to cover Shannon's where it rested on his arm. "My wife is wearing that ring, now."

She'd known he'd given her his mother's wedding ring, but it felt odd now to have Mr. Pearson's gaze drop to her hand, as if to verify. She was so used to people staring at her cheek, that having one staring at her finger felt... almost funny.

The other man swallowed tightly. "She was a good woman, Lucas, and would want your bride to wear her ring. We're all going to miss her."

"Me too." Her husband sighed, and Shannon resisted the urge to pat *his* hand, not sure if he'd approve of her comfort in front of his friend. "And I think you're right." He sent a sad smile towards Shannon, and his fingers tightened briefly around hers. "She'd be pleased with my choice in a wife."

The late Mrs. Ryan would've been pleased with *any* bride her son had chosen, Shannon thought. But one who'd hidden the truth about herself? It was hard to imagine any mother approving of *that*.

But then, Lucas's mother had urged him to marry and produce an heir, which meant *she* had been aware of whatever threat faced Lucas and Sunset Valley. Shannon sighed and acknowledged she didn't have her husband's heart, nor his trust. It would be silly to bemoan the fact now, when Mr. Pearson was trying so hard to be solicitous.

So she smiled politely at his attempts at flattery, and gritted her teeth until he left with the key to fetch whatever Lucas's mother had locked up here.

As soon as he was gone, Lucas turned to her, concern on his face. "Shannon, honey? Are you alright? Do you want to sit down?"

"Me?" Goodness, did her smile really look that fake?

"You're the one I should be asking that of." She twined her fingers through his where they still rested in the crook of his other arm. "I'm so sorry I didn't have a chance to meet your mother."

His lovely golden-brown eyes flicked across her face, as if searching for the truth, and she forced a serene expression. He couldn't know about the roil of emotions in her chest.

"I am too," he whispered. "But you looked awfully sick there when you met Mr. Pearson. I tried…"

When he trailed off, Shannon almost bit her own lip. "Oh, I'm alright," she forced herself to say breezily. "Just overly full from lunch, I suspect." The meal really *had* been delicious, and such a nice treat.

"Oh." He didn't look convinced by her excuse, and Shannon wasn't surprised. It hadn't been a very convincing excuse, after all. "I just thought, maybe…?"

"Maybe what?"

He shrugged. "Well, we're both hoping for a baby, after all, and you looked—"

"Here you go, Lucas!"

Mr. Pearson's return caused her husband to straighten swiftly, pulling back as if he'd been caught in a compromising situation. He recovered well though, and began chatting with the banker about the bundle of papers the older man held.

Which was good, because Shannon suddenly couldn't breathe very well.

Could she be pregnant?

She began to count in her head. Surely it was too soon to tell, wasn't it? Her fingers clutched at her husband's sleeve, and she tried to catalog her own body. Were her breasts more tender than usual? Her nose more sensitive to certain scents?

All those things were what Cora had described to her, when they'd discussed Shannon's dream of becoming a mother.

No, surely it was too soon to tell.

But Shannon's fingers crept across the cotton of her dress to press against her abdomen as she stared out the bank's window. It was too soon to tell, but maybe…

Maybe someday soon, based on how often she and her husband made love, she'd be pregnant.

And then she could turn her love to her baby. That baby would love her, no matter how she looked. And that baby would trust her enough to tell her all of his secrets.

And she could never, ever lie to that baby the way she'd lied to his father.

———

YEAH, there was something wrong with Shannon, alright. Lucas had watched her go all pale when she'd been introduced to Daniel, but hadn't been able to guess why. And then, the longer they'd stood there making small talk, the more her fingers had tightened on his sleeve, and he'd started to wonder.

Maybe it hadn't been too polite of him to just come out and ask if she could be pregnant. The center of the bank's lobby was hardly the place for it, after all. But instead of going all white again, Shannon had blushed and those pretty blue eyes had widened, and he'd seen genuine surprise in them when he'd hinted.

No, she wasn't pregnant, but she wasn't alright either, like she'd claimed.

They were back outside, walking towards the livery where he'd left the carriage. The June sun was beating down, and Lucas wracked his brain to try to come up with some way to broach the subject.

"It's a nice day." He winced, knowing his words were stilted. "You want to sit down and rest a little bit?"

Her eyes followed his pointing finger toward the benches set under the apple trees in front of the church, but then she looked away and shook her head. Was it his imagination, or had she looked a little wistful there before she'd glanced at the trio of ladies who were already sitting over there and chatting? Didn't she say she wanted to meet other townspeople? Or had she just had enough of being social today?

Lucas didn't understand his wife and wished she'd open up and explain things to him.

But he didn't say anything. Instead, he just sighed and headed toward the north end of town once more, with her holding his elbow mutely.

When did things get so awkward between them?

She was definitely holding something back from him. For one bright moment, there in the bank, he'd hoped that maybe it was news of her pregnancy, but her reaction convinced him otherwise.

Oh well.

They were passing the sheriff's office, and only a few moments away from the rickety old schoolhouse, when Lucas tried one more time to come up with a way to get her to enjoy the town. Black Aces—which had been named for the winning hand in a poker game—had been a sweet little town up until a few years back, when Augustus King had moved in.

The man had been doing his best to take over the whole town, and had brought in a few thugs to enforce his rule. The sheriff was in his pocket, and already a few businesses had folded and left for greener pastures. But there were enough of the people Lucas knew left for him to feel comfortable showing Shannon around. Hopefully, she'd fall in love with the little town he'd grown up in, same as he had.

He nodded across the street to the dry goods store, which had a selection of ladies' hats in the window.

"Shall we stop at—"

Shannon's squeak of surprise slammed his attention back to their path, which was quite suddenly blocked. A man had stepped out from the alley between the sheriff's office and the blacksmith's shop, and now stood in front of them, uncomfortably close.

Uncomfortably, because this man was dangerous.

Lucas pulled his wife back a step, and uncharacteristically wished he was holding his rifle. He didn't usually wear guns, but if *this* was the sort of rabble Black Aces was attracting these days, he could see the benefit.

Was this another one of King's cronies? An employee of Pierce? A friend of Baker's?

The stranger sure looked as if he knew the notorious gunslinger. The older man—forty or thereabouts—was dressed all in black, and not the fancy black either. Just plain black, with no trace of trail dust anywhere except the base of his black boots. His jaw was hard, without a trace of a beard, and his eyes reminded Lucas of a favorite childhood cat; a brown light enough to be called topaz or gold.

But what made the man look so dangerous was the gun belt slung low over his hips. Lucas had never seen anyone besides Baker who carried two guns like that, but this man did; a big Colt Army revolver on his right hip and what looked like one of those new double-action, self-cocking Colts on his left.

Lucas vowed that, should the man's hands twitch

toward either of those guns, he'd toss Shannon against the building and flatten himself in front of her to protect her. Surely Sheriff McNelis would notice any shooting and head out here before Shannon could be hurt.

But the man's hands were nowhere near his guns. In fact, he had them clasped behind his back and stood loosely, those eerie eyes examining Lucas and his wife. He exuded danger, while not actually doing anything dangerous.

"Lucas."

The stranger's voice was low and quiet, and Lucas found himself nodding a greeting before he registered Shannon's gasp of surprise. Once he did though, he frowned.

"How do you know my name?" And why would the man use his first name, rather than his last? "Do I know you?"

There hadn't been a hint of a question in the stranger's voice, as if he'd known exactly who he was talking to.

The golden eyes flickered over Shannon, then met Lucas's once more, and the younger man wished he could read the stranger's face.

"I am Verrick."

The somber announcement might not have had the effect it usually did. Lucas let out his breath in a relieved *whoosh*.

"It's about time." He'd sent a telegram offering to hire the gunslinger a month ago.

But the man's monotone didn't waver when he made his excuse. "I've been busy. You didn't need me yet."

Well, he was right. Lucas *hadn't* been threatened, during the last month. Other than the evidence of someone— Two-Grins Baker, surely—camping on his land and watching the ranch, there hadn't been any danger. Still, it was galling to be told this by the man he'd planned on hiring for protection.

"Lucas?" Shannon's voice was shaky. "Aren't you going to introduce me to Mr. Verrick?"

Lucas didn't bother hiding his wince. How did one introduce his wife to the west's most notorious gunslinger? Verrick was said to have killed over fifty men in fair fights, and Lord knows how many others. But when Pierce had brought in Two-Grins Baker, Verrick was the only one Lucas could think to hire, and that was only because of his mother's urging.

What would a wife think, having a man like that living at Sunset Valley?

So he swallowed, and forced a polite tone. "Honey, this is the bodyguard I hired to discourage Pierce." And then, because he knew she'd expect it from him, he nodded to the gunslinger. "This is my wife, Shannon Ryan."

To his surprise, Shannon gave an abbreviated curtsy, and after a moment of staring at her, Verrick nodded somberly.

"Shannon," he acknowledged, and Lucas wondered again at the man's familiarity. He should've referred to them as the Ryans, but instead used their first names without permission to do so.

"A bodyguard, Lucas?" Shannon's fingers curled around his sleeve. "Mr. Verrick is here to protect you from Mr. Pierce's offers to *buy* the land, is he?"

Damn.

His little wife had definitely realized he was keeping something from her. She was not only lovely and caring, but smart as well. All those things swelled his heart with pride, but frustrated him in regards to this particular issue as well.

"I think…" He swallowed, glancing between the

woman he was coming to love, and the man who'd been hired to keep him alive. "I think we'd better head back to the ranch and talk things over."

And maybe once they were there, he could figure out what was going on with Shannon. Only problem was, he was beginning to suspect he couldn't just demand her trust; he'd have to show her *he* trusted *her* too.

Lucas snorted under his breath, as he steered Shannon around the eerie gunslinger and headed toward the livery. And here he'd thought marriage would *solve* his problems.

Chapter Four

O n the ride home, Shannon opted to sit up front with Lucas, even though the rear seats were comfier. *He* was sitting up front, and with the mysterious Mr. Verrick riding alongside on a coal-black horse, she didn't want to sit alone. Thankful for the small bench, she pressed the side of her leg against her husband, and took comfort in his strong presence.

She wasn't sure why Lucas had hired a gunslinger, and that's what worried Shannon. Oh, she'd heard of Verrick —Who hadn't? He was notorious, and not just for his kills. Her brothers used to talk about him as if he was some kind of devil, one who would kill a man as soon as look at him. They said the man was equally fast with either hand, and could carve a man to pieces with the large knife she'd seen strapped to the back of his belt.

And they said he was available for hire to whomever had the money.

Looking at him now, from the corner of her eye, Shannon could believe Joshua and Caleb's claims. Verrick was everything her brothers had said, and more. His golden eyes were hard, exactly the way she imagined a killer's would be, and his face never betrayed any emotion. In the time she'd been watching him, he hadn't smiled or frowned, or even twitched an eyebrow.

He was like some kind of clockwork machine, and he gave Shannon the willies. She pressed against her husband's side, despite the heat, and wondered what trouble he could possibly be in which required hiring such a man. No matter what her husband claimed, Shannon was certain Pierce was doing more than just offering to buy the land.

Why else would Lucas take a chance like hiring *Verrick*? Surely having America's most infamous killer on the ranch was going to be even more dangerous than any threat from Pierce.

With all of these thoughts swirling around her head, it was a good thing the ride back to the ranch didn't take too long. It seemed as if she'd barely had a chance to come to terms with the gunslinger's presence, before they were pulling up in front of the house.

Cora was on the front porch, despite the heat. She'd claimed one corner for her own, and Lucas hadn't objected to her setting up her easel and painting supplies where she could see the mountains. When she saw the carriage approaching though, she put down her brush and ambled over to the steps.

"Hello there! Did you have a nice time in town?"

Cora's smile was teasing, and Shannon might've blushed, had she not been so distracted by other worries. She'd confessed her excitement about spending so much time with her husband, and knew Cora would want to hear all about their time in Black Aces. But right now, all Shannon could think about was the fact her husband was in some kind of danger and hadn't shared the truth with her.

When all she offered was a sickly smile in return, Cora's expression grew serious, and Shannon saw her gaze dart across to Lucas. "Is everything alright?"

"Everything's just fine." Lucas's claim was less reassuring than he'd probably hoped, and Shannon wondered how he was planning on explaining Verrick's presence.

He apparently wouldn't need to. The gunslinger swung down off his horse and looped the reins around the porch railing just inches from where Cora's hand rested. The older woman didn't gasp or jerk back to Shannon's surprise.

As Lucas lifted her down out of the carriage, Shannon found herself watching her sister. Verrick ducked under his horse's neck and climbed the few steps to the porch. He stood in front of Cora, and Shannon saw those disconcerting pale eyes of his raking her from head to knee.

And then, again to Shannon's surprise, Cora did the exact same thing. Her entirely too-bohemian sister gave Verrick—a truly dangerous man—a complete inspection in return, and from the way one corner of her lips pulled up, must have appreciated what she saw.

"I'm Cora Montgomery, Shannon's sister." She stuck her hand out, as if expecting the gunslinger to shake it.

Instead, Verrick merely looked down at it, then back up at her. Without changing his expression—did the man *ever* change his expression?—his gaze flicked down to where Lucas and Shannon stood, Lucas's hands still on her waist, then across the yard.

It wasn't until his cat-like eyes swept across the rest of the property that Shannon understood; the man was looking for danger, even now. Did he not rest? Was he *always* expecting danger?

She sighed as Lucas herded them all indoors. If her husband was somehow in trouble from Mr. Pierce, then it was probably best to have someone like Verrick on their side. Someone who was constantly alert for trouble, and who had the experience to protect Lucas.

Having him stay on the ranch was going to be uncomfortable, but it wasn't as if they had to *like* the man. He didn't look like the kind of person who made friends easily...or at all.

Still, when Shannon met her sister's eyes, Cora smiled and raised one brow. Oh sure, Cora *would* see the west's most notorious gunslinger as a challenge, wouldn't she?

Shannon sighed and grabbed her sister's hand to pull her inside after Verrick. It was somehow up to her to be a good hostess, *and* explain to her sister who their new guest was.

And enlist her help in praying Lucas hadn't just invited a world of pain into their home.

———

"Lucas! Lucas? Lucas, you'd better come quick!"

Lucas looked up from where he was helping Sam and Lefty re-wire the fence, searching for the direction of the calls.

His foreman came tearing over the hill, tugging on the reins of a spare gelding. Lucas immediately straightened, pulling off his gloves. What was so bad that Blake hadn't wanted to take the time to wait for Lucas to fetch his horse? Was it Shannon? Was she hurt?

He was already jogging toward the direction of the house when Blake pulled his animal to a stop.

"What's wrong?" he asked his foreman, dreading the answer.

"Pierce is here, asking to speak with you."

A cold dread settled in Lucas's stomach. "Where's Shannon?"

"I don't know. That's why I came to find you."

Lucas cursed. That was exactly what he'd been afraid of. He took the reins from Blake and swung into the saddle, sending a look back at Sam, who nodded and pulled at his hat.

"We'll be fine t' finish up here, Mr. Ryan."

Lucas nodded, then kicked the borrowed horse into a gallop, Blake pounding along behind. Shannon was alone with Pierce? Why did that worry him so much?

Because Pierce couldn't be trusted, and he wasn't sure the man wouldn't harm her. He'd hired a gunslinger to intimidate Lucas, after all; there was no telling what he'd say to Shannon.

Lucas swallowed. Surely Pierce wouldn't invite Two-Grins Baker to this "neighborly" visit? Or was Lucas's wife even now serving tea to a gunslinger?

Lucas cursed again and willed the horse to run faster. He had to reach her, had to make sure she was safe.

The ranch was deceptively calm when he and Blake reined their sweating animals in front of the house. Lucas tossed his foreman the horse's reins and took the stairs up to the porch three at a time. He burst through the front door and into the parlor where Shannon and her sister enjoyed their afternoon tea, then rocked to a stop.

Joseph Pierce was sitting on a couch, his hat beside him, impatiently strumming his fingers on his knee. Shannon was nowhere to be seen, and Lucas forced himself to swallow down his thankful sigh. But standing behind Pierce was the man Lucas had come to dread.

Two-Grins Baker's smile was just as chilling as Lucas

had heard, and made the man instantly recognizable. Pierce had brought the devil himself into Lucas's home?

"Lucas!" Pierce stood up, slapping his hat against his thigh. "Where's that pretty new wife of yours? I didn't see her at church last week."

"That's because you weren't there." Lucas kept his voice hard, determined not to show his father's old partner he was nervous. "What do you want?"

Pierce *tsked*. "That ain't very polite, boy. I came by to be neighborly. And to get to know *Shannon* a little better."

Was it Lucas's imagination, or was Pierce only a few heartbeats away from licking his lips when he'd said her name? Hands clenching into fists on each side, Lucas forced himself to remain calm. Instead of answering, he raised one brow.

Pierce's disappointed expression was obviously faked. "Very well. I guess there's some people who just don't know how to be gracious. Come on, Two-Grins." He gestured to the other man, as if they were getting ready to leave, but then stopped suddenly. "Oh, I don't believe you've met my associate, Two-Grins Baker? I hired him to take care of some of my problems."

Lucas snorted. Problems? The man was a vicious gun-for-hire, and his presence had resulted in Verrick being at Sunset Valley too. And just where *was* Lucas's hired body-guard? Hopefully protecting Shannon, wherever she was, because he sure as hell wasn't here protecting Lucas.

Pierce watched him carefully, probably looking for signs Lucas was worried. But Lucas kept his expression blank—ironically, trying to mimic the way he'd seen Verrick look over the last week—and Pierce's cruel grin faltered slightly.

The older man turned to his gunslinger, pretending as if everything was hunky-dory. "Two-Grins, this is Lucas Ryan. That *problem* I was telling you about."

Well, hell. The man all but admitted he'd hired a gunslinger to "take care of" Lucas in Lucas's own home? "I'm not selling you the land, Pierce."

"Oh, that offer's not on the table anymore, boy." The older man wasn't pretending to be polite anymore. "But I will get that land."

The significant look Pierce sent in Baker's direction left no doubt in anyone's mind what he'd meant. Lucas's refusal to sell the land was a "problem," and Baker had been hired to fix it. And Two-Grins Baker only knew one way to solve a problem.

Baker was here to kill Lucas, and Verrick wasn't even around. What the hell kind of bodyguard was he, anyhow? Lucas swallowed and shifted, setting his feet firmly and wondering if he was about to be killed in his own home.

Pierce must've seen that his intimidation worked—apparently Lucas wasn't as good as Verrick was about keeping his thoughts hidden—because his lips twitched once before he pulled his hat back on his head.

"Give my regards to your wife, won't you, boy?"

"I'm not ever going to let you near her, Pierce, you've gotta know that." He hadn't even told her how much trouble Pierce could be; like hell would he have her *meet* the bastard.

"Oh…" Lucas's gut clenched at the way Pierce drew out the syllable. "I'm not the one she's got to worry about meeting, am I?"

It wasn't until he'd breezed past Lucas, and Baker had grinned that horrible grin of his, then followed his boss out the door, that Lucas understood what he'd meant.

"Son of a—!" He actually took a step toward the door, wondering if he could go out there and challenge Baker, before realizing how stupid that would be. He was unarmed—he'd been fixing fence, for God's sake—and had no idea where his wife and sister-in-law were. Better make sure they were safe.

He hissed another curse, and slammed his fist into his palm. That bastard had actually suggested Baker would go after Shannon! What good would *that* do?

"You showed restraint. Good."

At Verrick's monotone, Lucas whirled. His bodyguard was no longer absent, but currently standing in the shadows on the far side of the room. Had he been there throughout the meeting? Lucas wracked his memory; surely he would've noticed the other man?

He was startled, and still angry at Pierce, and said the first thing that popped into his head. "Where the hell have you been?"

Then he winced, wondering if it was smart to offend someone like Verrick.

But the gunslinger's expression didn't change. "Watching. I thought it best if they didn't see me and realize you hired your own protection."

Slowly, Lucas nodded, seeing the wisdom in the other man's words, even while wishing Pierce knew Sunset Valley had a protector. "And where's my wife?" he asked instinctively.

"With her sister upstairs." The older man paused, his expressionless gaze flicking towards the ceiling once. "I convinced them it would be best to retreat when Pierce arrived."

Lucas stared at the other man a long minute, wondering what a man like Verrick could do to *convince* two ladies of anything. He didn't want to offend, but he had to know. "Are they alright?"

Verrick's gaze snapped back to his, and he blinked. "I have no way of knowing. But I heard your wife's sister say something which resulted in giggles from Shannon."

"*Giggles?*" It wasn't a word Lucas had expected the gunslinger to know.

"It wasn't laughter. More feminine, perhaps?"

Did the man really not know how to identify different kinds of laughter? "You're odd as hell, Verrick."

In the shadows, the man's blonde hair seemed to shine as he stared at Lucas. After a long moment, Verrick nodded, once. "Yes."

With that agreement, all of the air *whooshed* out of Lucas's lungs, and he collapsed into one of the chairs. He was in *so* much trouble. Pierce wasn't even hiding the fact he was threatening Shannon, and all Lucas wanted to do was lock his wife in the house.

"What do you think he meant, about Shannon meeting Baker? He's not actually talking about *hurting* her, is he?"

Verrick settled back on his heels and clasped his hands behind himself, in as close to a *resting* position as the man got. "I suspect he is."

In the week the gunslinger had been on the ranch, Lucas had explained everything he knew about the dangers Baker represented. But this was a new one. "Why?"

"Because he wants the ranch. And if you have an heir, the babe's existence will hardly stop him."

The truth slammed into Lucas so hard, he gasped. "You think he'd *kill* Shannon? Kill our child, if she's carrying?"

Verrick stared at him, and Lucas willed the older man to admit he was merely guessing. That he didn't know for sure Shannon was in danger.

But when he spoke, his monotone was hardly encouraging. "Why not? He is willing to kill you to get what he wants."

At the impassive agreement, Lucas knew the truth. His

mother's scheme to save the ranch was useless. Having an heir wouldn't discourage Pierce; it would just be another person for him to kill to get the land. A tiny, helpless, innocent person. One who wouldn't even exist if Shannon were to die.

"Oh God!" He threw himself from his chair, intent on rushing upstairs and doing whatever he could imagine to protect her, but Verrick startled him yet again when the other man appeared between him and the door without seeming to move.

"Calm yourself. You hired me to protect you, and I extend that same protection to your wife as well."

"Forget *me*!" Lucas began to pace, wondering if it was too early in the day to fetch that bottle of his father's whiskey from the dining room. "She's more important. I can't let anything happen to her!"

Verrick just watched stoically, as Lucas ran his hands through his hair, then groaned.

"God forgive me! I married her, I dragged her out here, and now she's in danger?" He resumed his pacing. "I thought by marrying her I was removing Pierce's threat, but it's really the opposite. I just multiplied the number of people in danger!" Lucas felt as if his heart was trying to drop into his stomach. How could he do this to her?

"Agreed." Verrick moved toward the small table and sat in the wooden chair beside it. "That was not well-thought-out of you."

"It was my mother's idea." Even as he said it, Lucas knew it made him sound like a petulant child.

But to his surprise, Verrick met his eyes and nodded once. "Yes. She did not think her ideas all the way through either."

Opening his mouth to defend his mother, Lucas paused. He had to admit in this case, Verrick was right. His mother's plan was seriously flawed, and if Lucas had really considered what he knew of Pierce's character, he would've realized a wife and baby wouldn't stop the man. Maybe Mother had just been desperate for a grandchild and had used Pierce as an excuse.

When Lucas didn't respond, the older man nodded once, then removed a piece of paper from his vest pocket. Unfolding it, he beckoned Lucas closer.

The hand-drawn map he smoothed out on the table was a remarkable representation of Sunset Valley. It wasn't until Verrick removed a pencil from his pocket and began to label one of the property borders—the Pierce spread, in fact—that Lucas realized the gunslinger had been the artist.

"These are the most likely routes for Baker to take, were he to come directly from Pierce's property." He marked paths on the map as Lucas pulled out a chair to join him. "If he were to come from town, then these are the routes he would take. I propose we—"

"He's been camping out on my land. Not since you got here, but I think it's likely he'll just keep watching and waiting for a chance to strike from here."

Lucas pointed to one of the spots he remembered finding a campsite a few weeks back. To his surprise, there was a notation there already. Curious, he checked on the other locations of Baker's known campsites. They were all marked, as well as others Lucas and Blake hadn't noticed. Suspicious now, Lucas met Verrick's golden gaze across the table. "These were Baker's campsites."

"No, they were not."

Lucas worked his jaw. "They were yours."

It wasn't a question, but Verrick nodded once.

"You *spied* on my property for *weeks* before you made yourself known to me?" Why in the hell would a man who

57

was interested in making money do something so time-consuming and worthless as that?

The other man didn't respond, but just stared impassively back, refusing to explain. The muscles in Lucas's jaw ached to yell, to lash out at *someone*. But the part of him that recognized danger also knew this man wasn't Pierce, wasn't Baker. In the week he'd been working for Lucas, Verrick hadn't done anything to threaten the Ryans. He must have his own reasons for spying on them—maybe he collected information on *all* of his clients before he agreed to accept the jobs?

Finally, Lucas exhaled and sat back in his chair. "I knew Pierce had hired Baker, and when we found the campsites, we assumed Baker was keeping an eye on us. It was one of the reasons I sent that second telegram."

"I never received it."

One side of Lucas's mouth pulled upward in a wry grin as he raked his hand through his hair. "Obviously. Because you were already here." He focused on the map once more. "If those weren't Baker's campsites, then maybe things aren't as dire as I'd thought?"

"Unlikely." Verrick placed the pencil down, aligning it precisely with one edge. "But Pierce is the greater threat."

"What do you mean?"

"Baker is being paid by Pierce. The man only works for cash, so if Pierce were no longer a threat to you, then Baker would not be either."

That was a reasonable explanation, and Lucas had to admit he'd had the thought in the past that, if Pierce were to die somehow, all of Lucas's worries would disappear. But Lucas wasn't the kind of man to wish ill on someone else; all he wanted was to work hard and build his ranch up. He had no plans to threaten Pierce, hence hiring

Verrick for protection against Baker, who Lucas still considered the bigger threat.

So he narrowed his eyes. "How do you know so much about Two-Grins Baker?"

Verrick hesitated—out of character for him—and then said only, "We have had some contact in the past."

"'Some contact?'" One of Lucas's brows rose. "Did you give him that big scar on his throat, his second grin?"

"Yes." That was all Verrick said, before picking up the pencil once more. "Do you wish to hear my suggestions for defense of your home?"

Lucas sat forward once more, his finger on the map where the ranch house sat. "First, promise me you'll protect Shannon. She *cannot* be hurt in this, no matter what Baker tries to do to me."

Slowly, Verrick's intense gaze climbed up Lucas's finger and arm until the older man was staring into his eyes. His expression gave nothing away, no indication of what he was thinking, and Lucas swallowed, wondering what it was about his request that caused such focus.

Finally, Verrick spoke. "You love her."

It wasn't a question, but Lucas took a deep breath and nodded. "I didn't expect to, when I sent for a mail-order bride, but she's just about perfect. I know we've only been married a month, but I can't imagine living without her or that wild sister of hers." He sat up straighter, feeling somehow *freer* with the admission. "Yeah, I love her, and I'd do anything to keep her safe." He met the older man's eyes once more. "So you have to promise me you'll protect her."

Something he'd said had gained Verrick's approval, apparently. The gunslinger nodded once. "Agreed." And then he placed the tip of the pencil to the map and raised one brow, which was practically a speech from him.

Nodding in response to the unasked question, Lucas bent over the map. "Show me what we need to do then."

And as Verrick outlined his theories on how Baker would attack, Lucas tried to focus. But all he could think about was that he'd put Shannon in danger. He'd been the one to bring her here, just to get an heir. But now, her becoming pregnant would put her in even more trouble. Everything he'd prayed so hard for would just be reason for Pierce to hurt her. To *kill* her.

And here was Lucas putting all of his faith in a gunslinger he barely knew. Verrick was Shannon's best hope now, because Lucas couldn't lose her. He couldn't lose her laughter, her comfort, her beauty. Couldn't lose his wife.

Couldn't lose the woman he loved.

Chapter Five

Good thing it was summertime, or else Shannon would have to stay inside to throw up. This was the third morning she'd woken before Lucas—as usual, in order to start breakfast—swung her legs over the side of the bed, and was struck with a wave of nausea. And like the last few days, she'd thrown on her robe, rushed downstairs and out the back door, before she'd lost what little remained in her stomach. And just like the last few days, as soon as she'd had a drink of cold water, she felt better.

And now she fixed coffee for her husband, not sure if she should be ecstatic at what her symptoms meant, or devastated.

She was pregnant, and that's all she'd ever wanted. A baby! Her hand caressed the front of her robe as she fetched down the sugar. She was going to have a baby, who would love her unconditionally. It was what Lucas wanted too…and that's the thought which gave her pause.

He wanted an heir, that was the reason he'd married her. But once he found out she was carrying, how would he react? There'd be no more reason for him to reach for her in the darkness in their bedroom. No more reason for that slow grin he sometimes got when she caught him watching her rear end. No more reason for his teasing touches.

More than just the love-making, she'd come to cherish the way he treated her with respect and caring, and how he asked her opinion about things. He might not love her, but she was very much in love with him, and to have him put her aside now that she was carrying his heir would crush her.

When Lucas came downstairs, she made sure none of her thoughts showed on her face, and just gave him a smile. He returned it, but had been distracted since yesterday. Something had happened, but he wasn't telling her. As usual. It was hard not to be hurt when he blocked her out from important discussions, but she reminded herself she deserved it, lying to him like she had.

He *did* stop to kiss her gently, before patting her rear end and trudging out the back door toward the barn. He'd be back soon with eggs and milk for breakfast—and to finish his coffee—but in the meantime, Shannon could put together the rest of the meal.

She began to mix the ingredients for the biscuits Lucas enjoyed. They were also a favorite of Cora's, but they'd run out of the jam her sister preferred over the butter. Shannon made a note to remind Lucas to have more picked up next time he or one of the hands went into town.

She hadn't been into Black Aces with him since last week, when they'd gone to the bank. The townspeople had been nice enough to her during all of her visits, but they inevitably stared at her face. It might be best to just let Lucas go in without her so he wouldn't have to be seen with her.

She turned from the side counter and almost dropped the butter crock with a shrill gasp.

"Verrick!" Her other hand pressed against her chest, as if she could still her racing heart. "You startled me."

The gunslinger's all-black clothing blended in with the shadows by the backdoor. How long had he been standing there? And how in the world did he manage to move so quietly?

He raised a single blonde brow, as if to say "No, really?" and she found herself smiling at how obvious her statement had been.

"You're right, I'm sorry. But could you maybe work on *not* startling me next time?" Who would imagine she could tease such an infamous gunslinger? Certainly not her when she'd met him last week. But since he'd been at Sunset Valley—sleeping who knew where—Shannon had realized his reputation was based mainly on his attitude. The man never smiled or gave any sort of expression that she could see. He was hard and intimidating and not a little scary… but hadn't done anything that was actually *worrying*. In fact, he'd been polite and respectful to her and Cora both, and even towards Lucas.

Unfortunately, that didn't extend to conversation topics. "Whether you startle or not is up to you."

She exhaled and sent him a chagrined smile before turning back to the bowl. "Well, yes, but you could help by not sneaking up on me."

"I don't sneak."

She snorted. "You definitely sneak." She'd turned her back on *Verrick*, the man her brothers feared, and hadn't thought anything of it. "Perhaps you could try calling a greeting tomorrow morning so I don't scream and throw the butter at you."

"I would've caught it."

"Of course. But go ahead, and try." She was smiling openly now, at her biscuit dough. Would he be offended if he saw it? Would he realize she was teasing him?

"A greeting." Was that a hint of skepticism in his voice?

"Try a 'good morning'."

He moved into her line of vision, and Shannon struggled to control her grin. "The state of your morning won't change simply because I wish you a good one."

She didn't look up as she cut some butter into the mix. "Sure it will."

"I don't see how."

This time she let him see her smile when she met his eyes. "Because you can improve someone's day just by letting them know you *hope* they have a good day."

He stared at her for a while. The man was *good* at staring. Creepy, almost, with those gold eyes. Lucas's eyes were a few shades darker, but where his were warm and full of laughter, Verrick's were…*not*. The gunslinger might be handsome—blonde hair was incongruous on someone with as dark a reputation as he had—but his lack of expression and the coldness in his eyes made him far scarier.

"Your day would be improved if I wished it?"

She blew out an exasperated breath. "My day would be improved because I knew you *wanted* me to have a good day. Because you care about how my day goes! That's the whole point of the greeting."

His chin dipped. "Interesting."

She couldn't help the laugh which burst free then. "You're quite odd, Verrick. You know that, don't you?"

"Your husband said something similar yesterday, yes."

She laughed again, wondering if this good mood was really a result of teasing a dangerous gunslinger, or because it *was* a nice day, or because she was finally going to have the baby she'd been dreaming about. Humming, she began to slice the bacon to fry, then glanced up to see Verrick still watching her.

It was hard to tell, considering how impassive his expression usually was, but right now he looked…almost wistful.

Her knife halted. "Mr. Verrick?"

"Have you told him?"

Told him? "Told who? Told him what?"

"Have you told Lucas you're pregnant?"

Carefully, Shannon set the knife down, her heart pounding in her ears. How did he know? Had he seen her throwing up? "Is it that obvious?"

"No." Verrick shifted slightly, then inhaled. "He would want to know."

"I'm planning on telling him, just…" *Why* was she having this conversation with *this* man? "I'm just waiting for a good time."

Golden eyes flicked around the room as if looking for trouble. "You might not have the luxury of a *good* time."

Something about the way he said it made her even more nervous. "Is this about Pierce?"

"Two-Grins Baker is Lucas's bigger concern right now."

Two-Grins Baker! "Good heavens!" she burst out. "You mean there are *two* gunslingers hanging around?" When she saw his lips tighten into a thin line, she was quick to apologize. "No offense, Verrick, but one of you is enough for me."

When he nodded, she exhaled, her gaze coming to rest on the knife.

"You mean to tell me Pierce has hired the most notorious gunslinger in the west?"

"Second-most notorious."

In surprise, she looked up. "Was that a joke, Mr. Verrick?"

His monotone didn't change. "It was an attempt."

But she couldn't smile, not now. "Did Pierce hire Baker?"

"Yes."

His confirmation of her suspicions didn't make her feel any better. She'd been right! This is what Lucas had been keeping from her. Pierce wasn't trying to *purchase* the Ryan land, he was planning on killing Lucas so the land would revert to him. But Lucas thought by having an heir—her hand drifted to her stomach—Pierce would give up. Was he right?

"And is Baker here to kill my husband?"

This time, Verrick hesitated before answering. "Yes." He took a deep breath and met her eyes. "But I am faster."

Oddly enough, that boast *did* make her feel better. Pierce wanted Lucas dead and had hired the *second*-fastest gunslinger to ensure it. But Lucas had managed to convince Verrick to come protect him, and that was somehow comforting. Looking at Verrick now, standing in her kitchen, Shannon had the oddest feeling he wouldn't let any harm come to her husband.

"Thank you, Mr. Verrick."

He nodded once, then turned on his heel to walk out of the kitchen. She stopped him before he could disappear again.

"Would you like some biscuits? They'll be done in a little bit."

When he turned, she could tell she'd surprised him. "I've eaten already."

That wasn't unexpected; he hadn't eaten any meals with them since arriving at the ranch last week. But she just smiled slightly, then nodded to let him know she understood.

She *was* surprised when he turned to leave once more, but then hesitated and said, "Thank you."

It was the first time he'd thanked her, and though it didn't sound natural, it pleased her he'd made the attempt. "You're welcome, Mr. Verrick. We'll have you wishing us 'good morning' in no time."

He didn't respond to her teasing, but merely said, "Lucas will be back soon. Tell him."

"Tell me what?"

Shannon's attention swung to the backdoor, where Lucas was grinning as he wiped off his boots. His attention was on Verrick, who'd ignored the question and flowed silently into the dining room in that disturbing way of his. Lucas met her eyes and his smile grew.

"I brought eggs." Sure enough, he was juggling the milk pail and the egg box, and raised them both to show her. He reminded her of a little boy, eager for praise, so she laughed.

"Thank you. I'll have breakfast ready soon."

He placed them both on the table near her, then crossed to the basin to wash his hands. "I didn't know you and Verrick were on speaking terms. What were you talking about?"

Shrugging, she pretended great interest in pouring the milk into the biscuit dough. "We never have *long* conversations, but he's interesting."

"Are you sure you're talking about *Verrick*?"

She snorted at his pretended confusion. "I thought he was scary when we first met, but now I'm not so sure."

"Shannon, he's killed—"

"Oh, I know," she was quick to assure him. "And

maybe it's all just an act on his part, but I trust him. He seems like a good man."

"He's a gunslinger." She could tell from the sound of his voice he'd turned and was facing her.

"Yes." She pounded the dough harder than necessary. "One *you* hired." Silence from her husband. Could he tell she wasn't pleased? Good. "To protect you from the gunslinger *Pierce* hired to kill you."

"Ah."

"You didn't think I would figure it out? I'm brighter than I look, you know." She tried to hide the bitterness in her voice, but knew she failed when she heard him sigh. "I might be ugly, but my mind is—"

His arms wrapped around her, and she bit off what she was going to say. Part of her wanted to be angry at him for keeping secrets from her, but the other traitorous part was thrilled he still wanted to touch her.

"Shannon…" He turned her around so she was looking up into his golden-brown eyes. "Honey, I never thought there was anything wrong with your mind." He dropped a kiss to her temple. "And I dunno what you mean about being ugly, but you've got to know that's not the truth."

What?

Shannon tried to form a coherent response, but he trailed kisses down her left cheek, down that horrible birth-mark, and she suddenly couldn't think. "I…don't…"

"You're lovely, honey. Don't ever think otherwise."

He's just saying that because he likes what we do in bed together. Once he knew about the baby, would he still want to hold her? Would he still think she was lovely?

"I'm pregnant." The blurted admission stunned her almost as much as it stunned him.

Lucas reared back, his hands on her upper arms. "Are you… Shannon, really? Are you sure?"

When she nodded, a look came across his face she couldn't identify. She'd expected him to be happy, but there was a hint of fear there too. He pulled her against him then, wrapping his arms tight across her back as if he could anchor her there. Hesitantly, she inched her hands around his sides until she was holding on as well.

They stood like that for a long moment, and before long Shannon swore she could feel his heart beating in time with hers.

Finally, he stirred.

"You're pregnant." His voice was rough against her hair. "We're going to have a baby."

His reaction was so much like hers Shannon felt her lips curve.

"I've been saying this is what I wanted, but now—? I… I can't believe it. Now it's actually happening, and I don't know what to say."

Was it her imagination, or did he sound close to tears? As if he didn't know if he should be happy or worried either. Shannon pressed herself against him even tighter.

"That was my reaction too," she confessed against his shoulder, and felt more than heard his snort of laughter.

Then he pulled away, his hands back on her arms once more, as if he could keep her from running away. "You're sure, Shannon? You're going to have our baby?"

She nodded again. "Are you…pleased?" The blush climbed unbidden up her cheeks until she knew she glowed like a tomato, and she tightened her grip on his shirt.

Instead of immediately reassuring her, Lucas looked… hesitant. A pit opened in her stomach. *Oh God*, this was what she'd been afraid of. Now that she was pregnant, he would lose interest in her.

"Aw, honey, I'm sorry." Something in her expression must've given her away, because Lucas lifted her chin with a finger. "Of course I'm happy. I shouldn't have taken my time answering, huh?"

She was too busy fighting down the feelings of loss and emptiness to respond.

"Shannon, I'm sorry. I'm thrilled. Really." He lifted her chin even more until she was staring into his warm eyes. "We're having a baby. I can't believe it."

Part of her couldn't believe it either. She wanted to tell him that, to join in his celebration, but she wasn't sure if he really *was* celebrating, or if he was already thinking of ways to pull away from her now that he had what he wanted.

Oh, if only she hadn't lied to him months ago when they'd first written! If only she'd told him the whole truth so he would trust her now!

But she'd made her bed, and now would have to sleep in it.

Apparently whatever he saw in her face wasn't comforting, because his grip on her arm tightened. "Don't worry. Everything will be alright."

Would it? She heard herself make a noise that might've been a laugh, or might've been a sob, and she pulled her chin out of his grip to bury it in his shoulder once more.

"Aw, honey." He whispered a curse against her hair, then his arms wrapped tight around her once more. "I'm sorry. I'm sorry."

The rhythmic stroking of his hands against her back should've been soothing, but the comfort he offered her made her want to cry.

She was going to have the baby she always wanted, and her husband was a kind man whom she didn't deserve. And now that she was giving him what he wanted—

needed—there was no reason for him to continue treating her so sweetly.

But his hands kept soothing her, and she felt…*cherished.*

"I'll keep you safe, Shannon, I will." His hold tightened. "I swear. You and the baby will be safe."

Safe? It was too late for that. Her heart was never going to be safe now.

She loved a man who couldn't love her back.

Chapter Six

H e was going to be a Daddy!
Lucas was still walking around with his head in the clouds. He'd wanted this, had imagined it, but now, to hear it was actually happening? It was surreal.

Before, the idea of having an heir meant security and peace, but now…? Now, all he could think about was, in a few short months there was going to be a tiny little human in this world who was going to rely entirely on him for its safety and happiness and comfort. He was going to be a daddy, and that was much more important than just having an heir.

But as soon as Shannon had told him, he'd realized the truth: he would do *anything* to protect this helpless little person. That feeling had hit him so hard in the gut, he was lucky to have been holding on to her, or he would've had to sit down.

He was going to be a Daddy, and he vowed that he'd be a better father than his own had been. That wouldn't be too hard, he'd often thought, but he *knew* now he'd make it true. This little person wouldn't ever have to wonder how much Lucas loved him—or her—and wouldn't ever have to worry about living up to his expectations. He'd love his child as much as he loved his wife.

All of that realization and emotion and longing had hit him right in the gut when Shannon had told him about the baby that morning. They'd been arguing—of *course* she'd figured out why he'd hired Verrick, but what was that nonsense about her being ugly?—and then *Bam!* That news almost buckled his knees.

He was going to be a Daddy!

But she must've realized how much danger she was in. After all, she'd been smart enough to figure out Pierce wanted Lucas dead, so she must've realized—even though it had taken him far too long to figure it out himself—that she was in danger too. He'd seen the way her expression had fallen, and had just *known* it meant she was afraid. It hurt so damn much to realize not only had he put her in danger by marrying her, but he'd frightened her as well.

It was his fault, and the guilt made him feel about two feet tall.

So he was running away. Blake had brought word about a missing group of cattle, and Lucas was going to join his foreman and Sam and Lefty, to see if they could follow the tracks back to Pierce's land. If they could *prove* Pierce was re-branding his beef, then…

Lucas sighed, and dropped his forehead against the leather of the saddle he was strapping to the feisty little mare he preferred. If they could prove Pierce was behind all the trouble at Sunset Valley, then *what?* Nothing. He wasn't going to stop at threats, or else he would've quit by now. No, Pierce was too confident, with his men and his gunslinger and his history with Lucas's father.

Pierce wasn't going to stop, and Shannon was going to get hurt.

He groaned and knocked his head against the saddle once more, before straightening. He was going to have to speak with Verrick about his plans for Baker. Two-Grins *couldn't* be allowed to hurt Shannon and their baby. He just couldn't.

"I would caution you against leaving."

At the sound of Verrick's voice, Lucas swung around. Sure enough, the stoic gunslinger was standing—hands behind his back as always, all of his weight resting on the balls of his feet as if he was ready to spring into action—between the mare's stall and the stable doors.

Despite the heat, the man's black clothing was immaculate.

Where did he sleep? How did he manage to look as if he was going to church all the time?

"Why?" Maybe it was surprise at seeing Verrick pop out of nowhere which made Lucas sound so irritated. "I've got work to do."

"Trust your foreman to find your missing cattle."

It shouldn't have surprised Lucas that Verrick knew about his plan for the day. The man seemed to know everything going on around Sunset Valley. But the guilt of putting Shannon in danger—of making her so sad this morning when she realized it—made him mulish. "This is my land, Verrick. I'm going to make sure the ranch survives."

"And it is my responsibility to make sure *you* survive."

Maybe it was the blandness of the other man's delivery, or the fact the memory of the look on Shannon's face was eating up Lucas's insides. Maybe it was both, but whatever it was, Lucas pulled off his hat and slammed it against his thigh, in lieu of throwing something. Like a punch. He cursed long and loud, but it didn't seem to help.

And Verrick didn't even blink. "I swore I would protect both of you, but I can't do that if you leave the house."

"Forget me!" Lucas yelled, pointing through the stable walls toward the house. "Shannon is the one in danger. After this morning—" His voice broke then, and he stopped, ashamed of how he'd lost control of his anger and fear in front of this man. He swallowed, willing his heart to beat at a normal pace. "You've got to protect her."

"I'll protect both of you. All three of you."

Verrick's voice hitched slightly at the word *three*, but Lucas didn't care the man was finally showing some emotion, or that he seemed to know about the baby already. Of *course* he knew about the baby. Lucas had known about the baby for all of two hours, but Verrick seemed to always know everything about everything anyhow.

Lucas cursed again, even though he knew it made him sound petulant. How many times had his father told him he sounded like a sentimental fool when he'd gotten so angry he wanted to punch something? Father used to blame Mother's influence for making Lucas so emotional, but Mother had always said it wasn't a bad thing to care so deeply. Still, whenever he lost his temper so thoroughly and satisfyingly, he could remember Father standing there glaring at him.

The way Verrick was now.

Only, the other man wasn't actually glaring, Lucas realized. In fact, he looked... Well, Lucas had never seen Verrick with any other expression than his normal bland one, but right now his lips were actually turned down in a slight frown, and there was something *else* in those eerie golden eyes.

Knowing Verrick was watching—judging—him, forced Lucas to take a calming breath. He didn't feel any less guilty about what he'd done to Shannon, but he knew he'd be able to do something about it.

Pointing at the gunslinger with the hand still holding his hat, Lucas managed to keep his voice calm when he said, "I want you to find Baker and kill him."

"When he comes here to hurt you or your wife, I will kill him."

"*No.*" Lucas clenched his jaw until he heard a pop. He had to make Verrick understand. "No. Find him. Kill him. *Now.*"

The gunslinger cocked his head, which was about as much emotion as Lucas could hope for from the impassive man. "When you hired me, you explained I would remain here on the ranch, protecting you until the danger was past."

"The danger won't *be* past until Baker is dead!"

Verrick didn't even blink at Lucas's outburst. "You weren't this adamant when you hired me."

"That's because Shannon wasn't in danger then." Why couldn't he understand?

"Ah." Verrick took three steps closer. "You didn't care this strongly about yourself before because you didn't think yourself worth killing for, unless your life was actually on the line."

Lucas opened his mouth to snap a reply, but realized at the last moment Verrick was correct. The man who didn't appear to have any of his own emotions had just explained exactly how Lucas felt. So he shut his mouth and eyed the gunslinger warily.

Verrick had been watching and nodded when Lucas refrained from speaking. He looked...*approving*. Approving because he'd figured out what was bothering Lucas, or approving because Lucas had kept his mouth shut?

"You love her."

This time, Lucas scowled at Verrick's not-at-all-a-question. "You know I do."

"Then *you* kill Baker."

The silence stretched.

You kill Baker. You kill Baker.

Verrick's words repeated in Lucas's head, until he could think of nothing else.

Kill Baker.

Behind him, one of the horses nickered and the noise sounded loud in the still stable.

Kill Baker to protect Shannon.

"I can't," he managed to choke out. He'd never taken a man's life, and couldn't imagine doing it, couldn't imagine staining his soul like that…

But he loved Shannon. And he was going to be a Daddy. Surely, *surely*, that was worth a stain on his soul, to protect her? To protect *them*.

Verrick took two more precise steps, until he stood within arm's reach. Vaguely, Lucas registered the gunslinger's hands had fallen forward, to rest on the black leather of his gun belt, so close to the butts of the Colt and the smaller revolver. And just as vaguely, Lucas wondered when he'd stopped being afraid of this notorious man.

"Yet you expect me to."

Lucas met Verrick's eyes, but didn't understand his stoic statement. "What?"

"You expect *me* to kill Baker."

"That's your job!" *That's why I hired you.*

Verrick didn't quite shrug, but the twitch of his shoulder might have been the closest Lucas had seen to one. "You, however, are the one with the reason to want him dead."

"You have a reason too!" shouted Lucas, thinking of the sizable sum he'd promised Verrick by telegraph. He was ashamed at how frustrated he sounded, but unable to calm down enough to argue rationally.

But at his outburst, Verrick jerked forward, as if reacting to Lucas' pain and guilt. He held himself still for a long moment, then Lucas watched the other man inhale deeply and straighten.

Verrick's eyes—only a few shades lighter than Lucas's —seemed to pierce the feet between them. After far too many heartbeats, he inclined his head briefly. "Yes. I do."

Lucas exhaled. "I'll get the money—"

"Loving someone means you will do whatever is necessary to protect them."

Lucas scoffed and turned away, hoping to drown out Verrick's voice in his head. *You kill Baker.*

"Like you would know," he muttered under his breath. It was impossible to imagine someone like Verrick loving anyone.

But part of him *wanted* the gunslinger to defend himself, to tell Lucas who he had loved, and what he'd had to do to protect that person. Instead, there was only silence behind him. Lucas placed both hands on the saddle his patient mare still wore and wondered what he was going to do.

Verrick's voice, when it finally came, was way over by the door. That man sure could move silently. "Don't leave your wife today. I will stay nearby."

Ugh.

Verrick was right; Lucas couldn't leave Shannon. Not after what she'd told him that morning. Not while she must be so scared. He'd gotten her into this, and he would do anything to protect her.

It wasn't until he'd pulled the saddle off the horse and was standing there staring at a knot in the wood of the stable wall that Lucas realized exactly how he felt. He loved Shannon and *would* do anything to protect her.

Loving someone means you will do whatever is necessary to protect them.

Verrick's words echoed his own thoughts. And Lucas knew what that meant. It meant the gunslinger was right, and Lucas *would* protect his wife.

He'd never killed a man before. In fact, he'd always felt a sort of vague contempt for men like his father and Pierce and King, who could push around and intimidate other men. So a man who would *kill?* Lucas didn't want anything to do with that sort of man. Never wanted to *be* that sort of man.

But he'd do anything to protect Shannon and their unborn child.

Because that's what a father did.

Lucas swallowed and finished putting away his tack. It was time to accept the truth; if Two-Grins Baker came to the ranch to hurt Shannon, Lucas would become the man he never thought he'd be. He would kill Baker, if Verrick wouldn't.

Of course, Pierce was still the problem. Even with Baker out of the way, Pierce could still threaten Shannon. Maybe knowing Verrick was at Sunset Valley would discourage Pierce from trying another scheme to get the land?

But Lucas couldn't afford to pay Verrick indefinitely. The gunslinger hadn't discussed compensation, but Lucas had quoted him a high payment when he'd originally telegraphed, and Verrick had arrived, so surely that meant the price was settled.

Oh well. He could always ask Verrick what he thought after the immediate danger was past.

Because it was only a matter of time before Baker

showed up at the ranch to kill Lucas. And now he realized that pregnant or not, Shannon would be killed too. There was no way Lucas would let that happen.

He gave his mare one last pat, then straightened his shoulders. He had to find Blake and tell him to be careful while he investigated the missing cattle…then he had to go load his father's revolver.

When Baker and Pierce arrived, he'd be ready.

Chapter Seven

"Sooo? Are you going to tell me what has you so distracted?"

Cora's question barely cut through Shannon's concentration. She was focused on removing the cookies from the hot tray without burning herself, and thinking about the conversation she'd had that morning with Lucas.

"Distracted? I'm not distracted," she mumbled distractedly.

Her sister snorted. "You asked a question about my latest project, and you haven't listened to a word I've said, have you?"

Shannon looked up, focusing momentarily on the wall in front of her. Cora was right; she *hadn't* listened to her sister's answer. In fact, she couldn't even recall asking the question. So she shrugged, and once more bent over the hot sugar cookies. "Sorry. Are you still working on that landscape you were so excited about last week?"

This time Cora burst into laughter. "I swear, if this is what being pregnant does to your brain, I'm *never* going to try it!"

Shannon turned around indignantly, her hands on her hips and the cookies forgotten. "*You* know too?"

Her sister was sitting *on* the table, swinging her bare feet back and forth, and grinning proudly. "Not until you just confessed I didn't!"

Shannon rolled her eyes in frustration and snatched up the cloth she'd used to take the hot tray out of the oven. Unfortunately, when she threw it at her sister, Cora had the bad manners to snatch it out of the air—laughing uproariously—instead of letting it slap satisfyingly around her face.

"So it's true? You're finally going to have a baby?" Cora asked between laughs.

"Finally?" Shannon asked indignantly. "I've only been married a month."

Her sister's response was almost by rote. "Not that marriage has anything to do with it. But are you happy? Feeling okay?"

Shannon's expression softened, as both her hands met over her abdomen. "I am," she answered all of Cora's questions at once. She was going to have a baby, and she was thrilled.

Now, if only she knew her husband's true feelings on the matter.

"And Lucas?" Her sister could be irritatingly insightful sometimes. "What did he say?"

Shannon opened her mouth to respond, but thought better of it, and instead turned back to her cookies. After a moment of silence, which stretched too long, she finally answered, "He's very happy. This is what he's wanted for a long time, as well."

"Oh. Good."

Cora didn't say anything more for a long time. Then

Shannon heard her hop down off the table, and pad bare-foot across the kitchen towards her.

"Come here," Shannon heard her sister say from behind her.

She turned to her Cora, and found the older woman's arms open for a hug already. She pressed against Cora, grateful for the comfort, even if she wasn't able to explain the need for it. Cora, for her part, just hugged her, willing to offer love and support without an explanation. Her big sister's hands rubbed up and down Shannon's back.

"Loving someone is hard, huh?"

Shannon nodded against her sister's shoulder, willing herself not to cry.

"Well…" Cora sighed, then pulled away. "I'm happy for you, that you're going to have the baby you've always wanted. And I'm glad you've found a place here, where you love your husband and he loves you."

The comment jerked Shannon's attention to her sister's face. Lucas loved her? No, Cora was wrong. Lucas was glad he'd married, yes, but he undoubtedly would've preferred a prettier woman, one who didn't lie. But Cora had sounded so sure…

Her older sister smiled and nodded, and Shannon's heart gave a little flip. Could Cora be right? Could Lucas love her?

As if they'd conjured him, Shannon heard her husband's boot-steps on the rear porch. "Shannon?"

Cora patted her shoulder. "I'm going to steal a cookie or two and get back to work. My landscapes have been popular, according to Mr. Ward's telegrams, but I'm trying something new."

Shannon nodded vaguely as her sister pilfered two of the warm cookies from the counter behind her. Cora's paintings were popular back east, and she shipped them to a broker in St. Louis for sale. The money she brought in more than made up for her inability to cook, and her habit of getting lost in her art for days at a time.

Cora floated out the door toward the dining room just as Lucas stamped in, his hands and face still wet from the pump out back.

Inexplicably, Shannon's palms went damp, and she began to tuck all of her little flyaway hairs back into place.

Why was she so flustered? Just because her handsome husband was coming toward her? Just because he might *love* her?

Their kiss was, as always, special. Even the gentle brushing of lips they shared caused warmth to spread through Shannon, and she wondered if it'd be appropriate to wrap her arms around him and pull them even closer together.

Maybe he'd had the same thought, because when she opened her eyes it was to find his golden-brown ones piercing them. "How are you feeling, wife?"

Shannon blushed at both his name for her and the intensity behind it. "Fine, husband."

He smiled and ran the back of his finger down her cheek. Her left cheek, the one marred by that ugly birthmark.

Instinctively, she turned slightly so it was hidden from him...and watched the light in his eyes dim somewhat. He sighed and stepped back, running his hand through his hair.

"Well, you're stuck with me for the rest of the day." Without explaining why, he continued, "So I figured I'd keep you company and sort through that pile of papers from my mother's box at the bank."

Shannon nodded a little more enthusiastically than the announcement warranted, grateful for the distraction. She whirled away to pick up a plate and slid a half-dozen warm cookies onto it. There was just enough milk left from the pail he'd brought in that morning to pour Lucas a small glass. She placed both in front of him just as he sat down at the small desk in the corner, and he smiled thankfully up at her.

She left him in silence while she cleaned up from the cookie-making, but he wasn't having any of that. He began to talk to her about the papers he was finding as he sorted through them. There was correspondence from his mother's family—some of which he read aloud—which then led to stories about his cousins and relations back in Cincinnati.

When he began pulling out the legal documents, he even asked her advice once in a while.

He held up a particularly fat bundle and waved it at her as he opened it. "This is my father's will, I think." He glanced at the first page. "Yep. Real official-looking, isn't it?"

She let him read quietly for a few minutes, before joining him in reading over his shoulder. Thomas Ryan had left the ranch and land and all the goods to his wife Laura or to his son Lucas, "if the boy was of age." Since Lucas had been a few months shy of eighteen when his father died, Shannon assumed his mother had legally inherited.

She pointed to another thick bundle. "Is that your mother's will?"

When Lucas nodded distractedly, she picked it up and opened it to read. Sure enough, Laura Ryan had inherited the entirety of her husband's estate, and had managed it well. And she left all of it to her only child, Lucas.

"Can I ask a question?" She didn't want to disturb him, but something had been nagging her.

"Uh-huh." He flipped a few pages in his father's will.

"Do you know if your father and Mr. Pierce had a legal arrangement?"

Her question must've surprised him, judging from the way Lucas dropped his hands—and his father's will—and frowned at the wall in front of him.

After a moment, he flicked his gaze up at her, confusion still pulling his lips downward. "No. I mean, no they didn't. I know that for sure. I can remember my father saying it was a gentleman's agreement, that they'd inherit each other's land if either passed away. Since they used to be partners."

"So," she began as she placed his mother's will down on the desk beside his elbow, "your father's legal will—the one that left everything to your mother—that takes precedence, right? I mean, legally, Mr. Pierce doesn't have any claim to your land at all."

Lucas sighed, and dropped his head to his hand. "Nope." He groaned, then ran his hand through his hair.

Shannon's fingers itched to caress the back of his head, and she finally gave into the urge, kneading the tight muscles beneath his wavy curls.

Her husband groaned again slightly, then said, "But my father and Pierce were two peas in a pod. I mean, the way Pierce has decided he wants this land? Yeah, my father was like that too. If he saw something he wanted, he went after it, without question and with no regards to anyone he might hurt."

Shannon's fingers dug into a knot at the base of his neck. "He doesn't sound very, um... *Nice*."

Lucas snorted, his eyes still closed, and dropped his chin forward to give her better access. "Not at all. He used to berate me all the time because I wasn't *tough* enough, wasn't as strong as he was. Apparently, having compassion was a sign of weakness to him."

"I'm glad you didn't turn out like him," Shannon whispered, thinking of how blessed she was to have a *compassionate* husband.

"Me too. Once I realized what he was like, once Mother helped me understand, I did my best to be the opposite of him. I never wanted to command fear. I'd rather earn respect. He once told me a loaded gun was the best way to get what you want, but I knew even then I didn't want to be a killer." He paused, as if thinking about something, then shook his head. "I didn't see a good enough reason to be a killer. I wasn't going to be like him."

"But if Pierce is just like him…?"

"Yeah." Lucas sighed, then dropped his head back against the chair, catching her hand in his and bringing it to his lips. "Yeah, that's the problem. Pierce is a killer too, and he hires killers. But the law doesn't seem likely to stop him. The sheriff won't do anything until we can prove it's Pierce causing all this trouble, and he's covered his footsteps. I'm afraid…" He squeezed her hand, then looked back to the two wills in front of him. "I'm afraid by the time he does something the sheriff can't ignore, it'll be too late."

Like Baker killing Lucas.

Shannon swallowed, unwilling to think of that. Her husband was smart. He'd hired the west's *most* notorious gunslinger to keep him safe, and for some reason, she trusted Verrick. She trusted him to keep Lucas safe.

Her stomach clenched, and she forced herself to relax. *For the baby's sake, if nothing else.* Lucas was going to be okay. He *had* to be, so she could determine if there was any truth to her sister's claim. Did Lucas love her, or was she in love with a man who would be happy to put her aside now that she carried his heir?

Desperate to distract them both, she reached for another folded piece of paper. "What's this? More letters?"

Lucas exhaled, straightened, and took it from her hand. "Let's see."

She heard the forced cheerfulness in his voice, and wondered if he was looking for a distraction too.

"The handwriting looks familiar, but I can't place it…"

Absentmindedly, she stroked his hair while he read, thinking how much she enjoyed touching him, and how heartbroken she'd be if—

No. Stop thinking about it.

"Huh." Lucas was scanning the letter. "Looks like it's a letter from a friend or some—" He cut himself off with a curse and dropped the letter, jerking his hands back as if he'd been burned.

"Lucas?"

He continued to stare at the piece of paper as if it were a snake.

"Lucas, what's wrong?"

He didn't answer, but just shook his head once, twice. She picked up the letter to find out what had upset him so much.

It began "Dear Laura," then proceeded to update Lucas's mother on the sender's attempts to find work since leaving Sunset Valley. She read quickly, not sure what had Lucas so spooked.

She found it in the last two paragraphs.

I'm finding there aren't many men willing to hire an eighteen-year-old on the basis of his own word, but my skill with a revolver has proven my claims. Even now I'm being contacted by men who wish me to solve their problems in a more permanent manner. It isn't the future I'd hoped for, nor the one I spoke of with you last year, but I am surviving.

This will be my last letter to you. I don't wish to anger Thomas, nor to risk revealing your secrets to him. I suspect the name I am making for myself will be deemed useful, if you—or young Lucas— ever need to reach me. Despite our differences, you must know I will do anything to protect our son.

Give him my love,
Verrick

THE PAPER FLUTTERED from Shannon's hand and came to a rest on the desk.

Our son.

Lucas's palms were flattened against the desk as he stared at the wall.

Our son.

Verrick had written a letter to Lucas's mother twenty-two years ago—the date had been scrawled across the top in strong handwriting—referencing their mutual son. He could've only meant Lucas.

"Maybe…" Shannon swallowed. "Maybe it's a different Verrick?"

Her husband's bark of laughter was harsh enough to make her wince. "There's only one Verrick, Shannon. Besides, I recognize his handwriting from the maps he made."

"But he's not that old. How could he possibly—"

"He's old enough, if he was eighteen when—" Lucas dropped his forehead to his hands. "My father… Oh my God. My father isn't really my father? How could Mother — *Why* would Mother…?"

Shannon felt her knees go weak as she understood all

the implications. Verrick was a handsome man, for all of the cold aura of deadliness he wrapped around himself. But what would he have been like when he was young? Younger than Lucas, at least? Had the late Mrs. Ryan been enamored with him? Had he taken advantage of her? The letter made it sound as if it had been a mutual relationship, but…

Verrick was the only one with the answers. Lucas was going to have to ask him. *Talk* to him. Find out the truth, if he could be trusted to give it.

She crossed to the table where Cora had been sitting earlier and gratefully leaned against it. Her stomach fluttered, and she wondered if she was going to lose her last meal. Again.

Lucas was Verrick's son. Everything they'd thought they'd known about the ranch, about his inheritance, was wrong.

Suddenly, Lucas slapped a palm against the desk, and Shannon's attention jerked back to her husband. "No! My mother wouldn't betray my fath—her husband like that! She wouldn't have *willingly*…" He trailed off as his eyes—only a few shades darker than Verrick's—met hers, seeking reassurance. "Would she?"

But Shannon could only shrug, sorry she couldn't give him more. "I don't know. If he had—had *forced* her, then he surely wouldn't have stayed on the ranch long enough to know about you, and I doubt very much he'd have written at all." The letter was dated six months after Lucas's birth. "And he certainly wouldn't have sent you his love."

His eyes closed on a curse, and she knew he saw the truth.

"How could she have done that?" he whispered, and her heart broke a little for him.

No matter the state of her knees or her stomach, her husband needed her more. She crossed back to his side. Without even looking up, he snaked his arm around her middle as soon as she drew within reach, and pulled her against him.

The breath squeezed out of her, Shannon could only stroke his hair as Lucas buried his face against her belly.

"Everything I thought I knew…"

"This doesn't change who *you* are, Lucas," she whispered. "You're still my husband. The father of my baby." He squeezed her a little tighter. "The man I—" She swallowed. "The man we all respect and admire."

"My father is a gunslinger." His voice was muffled, and her lips quirked a little.

"Yes, but a *handsome* one."

He stirred, and she found herself wanting to tease him a little.

"I didn't fully realize it before, but you have the same eyes, and jaw, even though *you* smile a lot more." She could think of a half dozen other ways the two men looked alike, from the shape of their shoulders, to the way they carried themselves when they walked, but he didn't need to hear all that at the moment. "You *do* resemble him, and I'll be happy if you looked that good when you're forty."

He pulled away slightly to glare at her, and she was able to kiss his forehead.

"I'm sorry, Lucas, but you *were* just telling me how dissimilar you were from your fa—from your mother's husband. And how you didn't want to be anything like him."

"I said I didn't want to be *feared*. Verrick is a killer—the most feared man in the west!"

Shannon struggled to make him understand, even though she herself couldn't truly understand it. "He is honorable though. I trust him. I don't think he *wants* to be feared—"

Lucas pulled away from her with a curse, and she felt as if part of her heart had been pulled away too. She'd rather have his love—well, if not his love, then at least his good will—than defend Verrick. "Lucas…"

"He's a killer, Shannon. Heartless and cruel, and I don't want to be like him." Lucas pushed against the desk and stood, knocking the chair over behind him. "I don't want anything to do with him!"

"I understand the way you're feeling, husband, but—"

"*How?*" Lucas spun back to her. "How am I feeling?"

Folding her hands in front of her, Shannon took a deep breath and tried to stay calm in the face of his anguish. "Angry. Betrayed and confused. Hurt, I imagine."

When he didn't reply, but just stood there, breathing heavily, she pushed on. "I understand this information will take some getting used to, but you're not alone, Lucas. Your past doesn't define you, and your parentage certainly doesn't."

She watched as the muscles in his jaw loosened slightly and the look in his eyes turned a little less angry. Hesitantly, she reached out to clasp his arm. "Verrick is the one with answers, Lucas. I know you don't want to talk to him about this"—she could see the distaste in the curl of his lip—"but it's the only way to understand, if that's your goal."

"I don't want to *talk* to him, Shannon."

She wondered at the emphasis. Did he want to *hit* Verrick instead? *Hurt* him? *Ignore* him?

"He's worse than my fath—the man I *thought* was my father! He's killed dozens of men, *for money!* How could I possibly look him in the eyes, knowing I'm his son? How could I respect *him?*"

There was a noise from the doorway. Shannon and

Lucas both swung around to see Verrick standing there in his usual impeccable black, his thumbs hooked on the front of his gun belt, his hat pushed up on his forehead.

His face was his usual unreadable mask, but his eyes… Shannon saw the pain there. If Lucas had wanted to hurt Verrick, he'd succeeded.

The older man didn't say anything, or acknowledge their presence or comments. Instead, he turned on one heel and strode away toward the front of the house.

Shannon watched her husband watch his father leave. Lucas's expression was a mixture of guilt and anger, and she wasn't sure how to make it better. All she knew was that the man who had raised Lucas had never shown him affection. And because of the type of man Thomas Ryan had been, Mr. Pierce thought he had a claim to Lucas's land, which is why Verrick was here in the first place.

Wasn't it?

She took a deep breath, and touched his hand. When his attention swung her way, she forced a small smile. "I don't have any answers, Lucas, but I *do* know that—at one time, at least—Verrick loved you. That's worth something."

Her husband stared down at her for much longer than her comment warranted, and she could see he was thinking. Remembering something which had passed between him and Verrick? Or could he see the love she felt for him?

Finally, he drew himself up, and nodded, glancing once more toward the door. "Should I…should I go after him?"

The hesitation in his question nearly broke her heart. She saw, simultaneously, the young boy yearning for his father's affection, and the man determined to do the right thing. Was the right thing to focus on God's commandment about not killing? Or to remember God alone could judge a man? Or was it to recognize sometimes there are exceptions, and to try to understand what drove a gunslinger to become the man he was?

So Shannon just shrugged and resisted the urge to wrap her arms around her husband to keep him safe.

Lucas grabbed her hand though, and raised it to his lips for a kiss. For a moment, she could pretend he *did* love her as much as she loved him, and she smiled. But when he dropped her hand and brushed past her, heading for the door his *father* had disappeared through, Shannon remembered the truth.

Her husband's world was crumbling, between Baker's threats and his mother's letters, and she was just a distraction. Shannon wrapped her arms around her middle—around their child—and blinked back tears.

Their baby would be Verrick's grandchild, and she wondered what that would mean. For Lucas's sake, she hoped the danger from Pierce and Baker could be resolved quickly and safely, so that they could figure out this mess.

Chapter Eight

"Verrick!" Lucas called when he strode out of the dining room. The older man stood before the front door, his way blocked by Cora. At Lucas's call, both of them started guiltily, and Lucas realized her hand was on Verrick's cheek. What had Lucas interrupted?

Verrick didn't look back, but brushed around Cora and slipped out the door in his usual silent way. Lucas took the time to stop and peer at his sister-in-law.

Cora's hand dropped to her side, and she smiled sort of sadly. "He's hurt, but he won't say—"

"I know," Lucas snapped, then winced.

Cora wasn't the one he was mad at. Neither Verrick, for that matter. He didn't know *who* he was mad at, but he knew he had to find the man and talk to him about…about *everything*.

Who *was* he?

Lucas had grown up hearing stories about Verrick the gunslinger from his mother. His mother, who'd obviously betrayed her marriage vows with the man when he was younger than Lucas was now. And it had been his mother who, months ago when they'd heard rumors of Pierce advertising for hired guns, had suggested he send for Verrick, the most feared gunslinger in the west.

The gunslinger who'd once told her he'd always be willing to protect their son.

Loving someone means you will do whatever is necessary to protect them.

Lucas groaned when he remembered Verrick had never discussed accepting payment for this job. He wasn't here for pay…he was here for *Lucas*.

"Verrick!" he called again when he burst out the front door.

But the porch and yard was empty, and while the gunslinger could probably take one look at the dust in front of the walk and know who'd gone where and how long ago, Lucas was hopeless. He took off for the stable at a jog, wondering if he'd driven the man off already.

Loving someone means you will do whatever is necessary to protect them.

He called again in the stable, not really expecting an answer and not receiving one. Verrick's big gelding was still in his stall, his tack still hanging undisturbed. Verrick hadn't ridden away.

"Verrick?"

Still no answer.

Where had the man gone? Where would he go when he'd just heard his son say that he'd never respect a killer?

Lucas winced and ran his hand through his hair in exasperation. He *couldn't* respect a man who killed others for a living, but that hadn't stopped him from *hiring* one as soon as there was a need. Was Verrick just a tool, who'd been used by others too unwilling to take care of their own problems? Was that what Lucas himself was doing now?

And how had that shaped a man who'd been doing it since he was eighteen?

And—*Oh God*—why did Lucas have to find that letter *now*? Today? On the day he discovered he was going to become a father? He'd always vowed to be a better father than his own had been, but come to find out, Thomas Ryan wasn't his father at all.

It would be a damn sight easier to be a better father than Verrick had been, that was for sure.

But in the back of his mind, Lucas reminded himself Verrick hadn't had the chance to be a father. What kind of father would he have been if he had?

Lucas muttered a curse. Standing here in the stable, with Shannon and Cora unprotected in the house, and Verrick only God knows where, wasn't going to help.

"Verrick, where the hell are you?"

Lucas stepped out of the building, wondering if he should find someone to go fetch Blake and the others back to the ranch. But when he saw the man with one foot poised to climb the steps to the house, Lucas began to run.

Pierce must've heard him, because he turned, his rifle tucking smoothly against his shoulder as he shifted his focus to the man tearing across the yard toward him.

Dimly, Lucas realized Pierce meant to shoot. Shoot Lucas, while standing practically on his porch!

The *bastard* had the audacity to step onto *his* land, to come to *his* home, with a loaded weapon? A weapon that, even now, was taking aim at Lucas's head?

Some sixth sense told Lucas to dive to the side just as Pierce squeezed the trigger, and the bullet blew his hat off instead of going through his chest. He turned the dive into a roll and came up just as Pierce was chambering another round.

And all of the anger, and frustration, and guilt he'd

been carrying around for the last few days finally caught up to him. "*Shannon is in there, you bastard!*" he yelled, launching himself at Pierce.

Time slowed as the older man swung the Winchester toward him, but Lucas wasn't thinking about the way the bullet would feel when it slammed into him, or the realization maybe he'd inherited some of his real father's instincts after all.

No, all he was thinking about was Shannon and their baby, and the knowledge with Verrick gone, *he* was the only one standing between the ones he loved and this monster.

Ironic that, despite both of them calling in gunslingers, it came down to the two of them, after all.

When Lucas slammed into Pierce, the Winchester was caught between them. The older man squeezed the trigger even as Lucas's arms wrapped around his middle and threw them both to the ground. Dimly, Lucas felt the burn under his arm as the bullet exploded out of the barrel, but it could be ignored in favor of making Joseph Pierce pay.

The two men rolled in the dust, but Lucas was younger and stronger. He yanked the Winchester out of Pierce's grip and tossed it as far away as he could from his prone position, then whipped his face out of the way of Pierce's fist. The blow caught him on the ear instead of the eye, making his head ring.

Lucas shook it off and bucked Pierce to the side, his hands already reaching for the other man's throat. He slammed Pierce's head into the ground once, twice, then *oof*ed in surprise when the older man levered him to one side and rolled towards the rifle.

"No!" he yelled and yanked Pierce back by the collar. "You're not going to hurt her!"

He was panting when he slammed his fist into the older

man's kidney, but it was an awkward blow, with him on his back. When Pierce merely grunted and reached again for the rifle, Lucas forced himself to roll to his knees. Everything seemed to hurt, but he couldn't, *couldn't* let Pierce grab that rifle again, couldn't let him climb the steps to hurt Shannon.

Loving someone means you will do whatever is necessary to protect them.

He wasn't a killer, but he wasn't going to let Pierce near Shannon either.

When he threw himself at the man who'd been bedeviling him for years, Lucas's hand found Pierce's throat. As he squeezed, he thought of Shannon, helpless inside the house, and what would've happened if Pierce had gone inside with his Winchester while Lucas was in the stable. What could, even now, be happening with Pierce's gunslinger, Baker, still on the loose.

Fear gave him strength, and he slammed Pierce's head into the ground.

I love her. I love her. I love her.

It felt like a million heartbeats until the man's angry snarl turned purple, then slack, and his cold eyes rolled back in his head.

But it wasn't until Pierce went limp beneath him that Lucas inhaled for the first time since tackling the man, and realized what he was doing. He was bleeding and dirty, and sore as hell, and choking the life out of another human being.

Cursing, he threw himself off Pierce and wiped his hands as if he could rid them of a killer's stain.

Loving someone means you will do whatever is necessary to protect them. But did that mean having to become a killer? A killer like his father?

Kneeling there in the dirt beside the body of the man

who'd come here to hurt Shannon, Lucas stared at his hands.

Were they the hands of a killer?

———

THE EXCITEMENT of the day must've made Shannon jumpy, because when she heard the sound of boots on the front steps, her gaze jerked to Cora's.

"Is that what I think it is?" she whispered. Both Lucas and Verrick had disappeared out the front door, but the sound of their steps wouldn't cause a pit of dread open in Shannon's stomach the way these did.

Her older sister was already reaching for the front door. "You stay here. I'll check."

Muttering a rude word, Shannon ignored her sister and tried to slip out the door too. The taller woman blocked her.

"I'm sure everything is fine out there, Shannon, but for the baby's sake you should stay safely in here. Verrick was very clear you could be in danger if you leave the house."

Her sister's cheeks were surprisingly flushed. What had happened in the foyer, before Shannon had finally decided to follow her husband out of the kitchen?

Shannon jabbed a finger in her sister's chest. "You might be older, and you might think you're wiser..."

Cora actually backed up a step, bumping against the door and looking surprised.

"...and you're definitely bigger than me." Another jab. "But if you think you can keep me from my husband when he needs me, you're about to learn differently, missy."

Her dark brows rising in surprise, Cora had the audacity to smile. "And what makes you think he needs you?"

As if in answer to her question, a gunshot rang out front, and both women frantically reached for the door at the same time.

Shannon slipped through first, just in time to see her husband lunge toward an older, gray-haired man who was trying to aim a rifle at him. Shannon's heart tried to climb up her throat. That *had* to be Mr. Pierce, because it certainly wasn't Two-Grins Baker.

The gun spat again, and she *felt* the bullet whiz past her and inside the house. Behind her, Cora squeaked and the sound of breaking glass followed, then Verrick appeared at Shannon's side.

She didn't know where to look. Her husband and Pierce were grappling on the ground, grunting and cursing, but Verrick's strong grip on her upper arm drew her attention to him. There was something in his eyes she'd never imagined seeing there.

It was fear.

"Take this." He slapped something in her palm, and her fingers automatically curled around the metal. "I have to find Baker."

It wasn't until he'd slipped around the side of the house, silent as always, that Shannon looked down to see that he'd given her the smaller of the two guns he always carried. In a daze, listening to the two men snarling on the ground, Shannon wondered if that meant Verrick trusted her.

"No!"

Her gaze snapped up at her husband's anguished cry.

"You're not going to hurt her!" Lucas grabbed Pierce and the two men tumbled back to the ground.

With trembling hands, Shannon lifted the small revolver, her finger curling through the trigger guard as she tried to train it on Pierce. She didn't want to hurt anyone, but she would, if it meant helping Lucas.

For now, though, her husband seemed to have the advantage. She watched him straddle Pierce, watched him lift the other man by the neck and slam him against the ground. Her stomach turned to see Lucas in so much pain he would do this to another man. He'd spent a lifetime determined not to be a killer, not to be like Thomas Ryan or Joseph Pierce.

And now…

"I love her!"

Shannon blinked. Surely she had misheard him?

"I love her. I love her." With each blow, Lucas's grunted confession seemed to rip out of him. "I love her!"

The rest of the world ceased to exist, overpowered by the frantic drum of her pulse in her ears and the tightness in her chest. *I love her.* Surely he wasn't talking about *her*? Surely she was mistaken?

I love her.

With a clarity that swept over her and weakened her knees, Shannon knew. Lucas *was* talking about *her*. He was trying to kill Pierce with his bare hands to protect *her*.

The revolver was suddenly too heavy, her palms too slick to do any good. She stumbled against the railing, dropping one hand to support herself and vaguely wondering what good she could possibly do for her husband in this state.

He loved her? After the way she'd lied to him, after all the secrets he'd been keeping from her, he loved her? He loved her as much as she loved him?

It wasn't until black began to creep around the edges of her vision that she realized she was holding her breath. Sucking in a great lungful, she focused on her husband once more. He was still now, kneeling in the dust beside the motionless body of the older man, staring down at his hands.

He loved her, and he'd just become someone he didn't want to be to save her. The enormity of his sacrifice made Shannon whimper, and in the silence, it seemed unnaturally loud. His golden-brown eyes met hers, and she shuddered at the bleakness she saw in them.

"Lucas," she whispered, then smiled. "Lucas, it's over."

His eyes widened slightly, and she knew she could help him. She forced all her love, all the comfort she could offer him into her voice, and stretched out one hand to him. "Come home, husband."

Come home to me. To our baby.

Maybe he understood, because he blinked once and forced himself to his feet. She saw him glance at his hands once more, before taking a deep breath and shaking his head. Her smile still in place, Shannon beckoned.

Come home to me, Lucas. No matter what he'd done, or who he'd become, she would still love him.

And then she realized her husband *hadn't* become a killer, because behind him, Pierce's questing hand had reached the rifle Lucas had flung aside. Shannon hadn't even seen the movement, but the man wasn't dead.

Not only wasn't he dead, but he was now levering the rifle toward her husband's back.

So she did the only thing she could do. She loved Lucas and would protect him the way he'd protected her.

"*Lucas!*" she shouted as she raised the revolver.

He *would* come home to her.

Chapter Nine

"Lucas!"

It wasn't until he saw her lift the gun—*where* had she gotten a gun?—that Lucas realized something was wrong.

Well, he'd known there was a hell of a *lot* wrong, but somehow it hadn't seemed to matter anymore when he'd looked up to see her on the porch.

She'd smiled at him, and he'd been drawn to her like a starving man. She was everything that was good and right in his world, and she was calling him home. The blood on his hands hadn't mattered when she smiled at him like that.

But then her expression had changed—fear?—and she'd screamed his name and lifted the gun, and that's when Lucas knew everything was about to go wrong.

Seriously wrong.

His instinct was to turn, to see if Pierce was still a threat, but he knew he didn't have time. He would have to trust her.

So he met her terrified eyes, saw the determined tilt of her jaw, and threw himself to the side.

Three gunshots, almost simultaneous, and time slowed.

He grunted when he felt one round tear open the flesh of his upper arm from behind.

One.

Must've been from Pierce's rifle—When had he grabbed it?

Shannon's revolver had spat flame as well. *Two.*

But where had the third shot come from?

Then he hit the ground.

Pain flared in his side where he'd been burned by the rifle, and in his arm where he'd been shot. Was the bullet still in there? Impossible to tell.

Was Pierce dead, or did he need to worry about rolling out of the way of another bullet? Getting dirt in the wound would be a small price to pay for staying alive.

Without even having time to groan, Lucas dragged his eyes toward the house. Shannon was still standing on the porch, still holding the revolver in both hands, still looking shocked as hell. Her delicate frame seemed to shiver, and her birthmark stood out against her abnormally pale skin.

Was she about to faint?

When Cora appeared behind her, Lucas knew his wife would be fine, but *he* needed to hold her. She'd saved him! She'd shot Pierce.

As he heaved himself to his knees, Lucas glanced at his enemy. Yes, Pierce was dead—there was a big hole in the man's chest.

She'd done that? God, his sweet little wife had *killed a man*? For him?

This time he *did* groan, thinking what it would mean to her to have done that.

Loving someone means you will do whatever is necessary to protect them.

Verrick's words echoed in his head. Shannon had protected him. Did she love him?

His vague musings were cut off when someone grabbed him from behind—his uninjured arm—and wrenched him to his feet. He tensed to defend himself, but when his unknown assailant spun him around, he relaxed.

It was Verrick.

"Lucas!"

That was all he said, but it was enough. The other man grasped him by his shoulders, his grip tight enough to make Lucas wince, but the relief in Verrick's eyes spoke volumes.

He'd been scared?

Scared for Lucas?

Remembering what Shannon had said about Verrick loving him once, and wondering if that meant he could still love him, Lucas forced a smile. "I'm alright. My wife saved me."

The older man was breathing heavily, his eyes skimming over Lucas, as if making sure he wasn't lying. But then he nodded, squeezed Lucas's arms once, and stepped back. He didn't say anything, and Lucas was glad for it. He wasn't sure how he felt about this man, and wasn't prepared to have to decide yet.

And then he wasn't thinking about Verrick, or Pierce, or Thomas Ryan at all, because Shannon had thrown herself off the porch and into his arms.

The rest of the world faded as he wrapped himself around her, not caring about the dust and the blood that covered him. He buried his head in her sweet-smelling hair and inhaled deeply, feeling the terror and tension ease.

She was safe. Their baby was safe. *He* was safe,

although it had taken a sacrifice from his wife he wouldn't have asked for.

Her small arms snaked around his middle, and he felt the fullness of her as she pressed her body against his. The body that would soon swell with their child, and would comfort him for years to come.

He squeezed his eyes shut and refused to think how close he'd come to losing her. "I love you, Shannon."

She pulled away just enough to tilt her head back and meet his eyes. She didn't say anything, but he could see her confusion in the way her brows tilted in and her lips tightened.

Didn't she believe him? Couldn't she see how much she meant to him?

He dropped a kiss to her forehead and suddenly felt inexplicably buoyant. He loved her, and thanks to her, he now had a lifetime to prove it. But—he tried to lift his right arm to brush away a strand of her hair, and instead winced in pain—maybe not right now.

"You're hurt!" she gasped, concern replacing the doubt on her face. "I didn't realize…" She was fumbling for his arm. "Let me see!"

Lucas's laugh was tinged with pain, but he couldn't help it. He was *alive*! "It's fine. *I'm* fine, thanks to you." He pulled Shannon against his side with his good arm. "You can fuss over me inside."

"Cora will have to help. Cora!"

Lucas followed her gaze to see his sister-in-law staring down at them from the porch. No, she wasn't staring at them, she was staring at Verrick. And interestingly, he was staring back just as intently. At Shannon's call though, Cora dragged her attention back to the embracing couple and raised a brow questioningly. As if she didn't see anything out of the ordinary about the last few minutes' proceedings.

"Are you alright?" Shannon asked. "I heard the bullet hit something behind me?"

Cora grinned. "I'm fine. Looks like we're all fine, actually." Her gaze flickered around the yard once, before landing back on Lucas. "But…"

Shannon stiffened. "What?"

"I'm sorry, but Pierce's second bullet, the one that, you know, zipped past us?"

The one that had burned its way out of the barrel against Lucas's side while they'd been grappling? Yeah, he knew, and found himself nodding along with Shannon to Cora's question.

"Well," she continued, suddenly looking rather concerned. "I'm really sorry, but it went in through the open door, and…"

Lucas tightened his hold on his wife. "What?"

"That vase that belonged to your mother? The one I moved to the little table in the foyer? I'm sorry, but it shattered that."

A broken vase?

A broken vase and a small hole in his arm were all they had to worry about from this misadventure? Well, that and a million bruises, but that was all. Things could've been much worse.

He felt the chuckles building in his chest, and didn't bother to stop the smile that spread across his face. When Shannon looked up at him quizzically, he squeezed her again.

"I always hated that vase."

She opened her mouth to respond, but hers wasn't the voice he heard.

"Me too."

Lucas's head whipped around at Verrick's bland agreement, and their eyes met in recognition of their shared opinion. Verrick had lived here at Sunset Valley years ago, after all. Lucas vowed one day soon, he'd sit down with this man and find out answers.

For now, though, they were all safe and the danger was past. The laughter built inside him again, and he wondered if this was just the aftermath of the shock. But Shannon's arms snaked around him once more, and he gave in to relief.

His arm might hurt like the blazes, and he'd been willing to become the killer he'd always despised, but his wife was safe beside him, and that's all that mattered.

Chapter Ten

"**M**ind if I join you?"

Shannon started at the sound of her husband's voice, but shifted over to one side of the porch swing, so he could slide in next to her. His right arm was resting in a sling, but his injury wasn't as bad as she'd feared, and she'd changed the bandages frequently.

It was sunset, three days after Pierce's death, and this was the first time Lucas had sought her out to be alone with her. Granted, for a lot of that time he'd been in bed—on her own orders!—recovering since his wound, but she couldn't help but feel the two were somehow linked. He'd declared his love for her, only to watch her become the thing he hated most. A killer.

Tonight though, he reached for her right hand where it lay beside him on the swing's wooden boards. He didn't look at her, but just watched the sunset and stroked his thumb over her palm, like he had all those weeks ago at the train station. She'd missed his touch *so much* since Pierce's death, but didn't have to guess at the reason he didn't reach for her in the night.

They sat in silence while the sun sank below the horizon, and when only the pink-tinged sky remained, she screwed up her courage and asked, "What did the sheriff say?"

The lawman had come out to the ranch today to speak with Lucas. He'd been out three days ago to collect Pierce's body, but both times Lucas had insisted he meet with the man alone. To protect her? Or because he was ashamed of her?

"That Pierce's funeral wasn't well-attended, and Baker hasn't been seen around. Also, after all those complaints I filed against him, the Sheriff and everyone else believe me that Pierce's death was self-defense."

"Oh." Neither of them looked at one another, but she twisted her hand in his grip until she could twine her fingers through his. "I'm glad to hear about Baker, but I wonder where he went."

"I don't know. But I'm guessing my—I'm guessing Verrick might know something about that."

A few moments of silence passed while Shannon worked up the gumption to ask what she'd been wondering for days: "Have you spoken to him yet…about everything?"

Lucas's silence was answer enough, but she saw him shake his head once. Braver now, she turned slightly on the swing, so she could see him. No matter his opinion of her, she *ached* for his pain and wanted to heal it as well as she'd sutured and tended to his bullet wound.

"I think you should invite him to dinner."

"What?" He glanced at her, then away. "Why?"

"Because he cares for you."

"I didn't think he could care for *any*thing."

There was a bitterness in his voice she didn't recognize, but understood.

"He cares for you. We all saw it after… Well, he was just as worried for you as I was. And I think, if you'd let yourself admit it, you'll see you want to care for him, as well."

"Care for Verrick? The west's most-feared gunslinger?"

Was it her imagination, or was there a touch of longing mixed in with his bitterness?

She smiled gently and waited until she could catch his eye once more. "Care for your father."

He stared at her, and after a dozen heartbeats, sighed. "You think he'd come to dinner with us?"

Trying to hide her exultant smile, she nodded. Then thought a moment and shrugged. "I don't know. But you can always ask."

"Huh."

She squeezed his fingers, willing him to agree. "I know you have questions—"

"Like if I actually own this ranch."

"What?" That hadn't been what she'd meant at all. "What do you mean?"

He shrugged too nonchalantly. "Sunset Valley is Thomas Ryan's ranch, and he made a deal with Pierce which was overridden when he married my mother and I was born. But if I'm not his actual son, maybe Pierce *should've* been the one to inherit…"

Horrified at the thought of Lucas torturing himself like this, Shannon shifted to face him. "Lucas, you *can't* think that. Pierce didn't deserve this land. Besides…" She swallowed, suddenly hesitant. "Verrick said…"

When she trailed off, he was the one to squeeze her hand. "Said what?"

"Did you know your father studied law at one point?"

"*Verrick?*"

She shrugged slightly. "I didn't ask details. But

yesterday he was in the kitchen while I was preparing dinner, and when I mentioned Pierce's claim to the land, he said you were the legal owner."

Verrick had stood there in the shadows of the kitchen, watching her work for several long minutes, before telling her he'd studied to be a lawyer in his youth. That had been a surprise, but also a relief when he'd continued his explanation.

"He said your mother was Thomas Ryan's legal heir, and you were *her* legal heir, so therefore the ranch belongs to you, regardless of your parentage."

Lucas was staring down at their joined hands. "He said that? The 'regardless of my parentage' bit, I mean?"

She nodded, even if Lucas wasn't watching. "I think he's unsure how to treat you—how you *want* him to treat you. I think he wants you to like him, but isn't sure how to build a relationship with you."

"That's why you want me to invite him to dinner?"

"Well, *that*, and so you can get some answers."

"Like whatever happened to Baker."

That hadn't been what she meant. Shannon opened her mouth to correct him, but then rethought it. "Well, yes. I guess." She and Lucas hadn't discussed that day yet, so he didn't know... "Verrick handed me his revolver, and then ran off, saying that he had to find Baker."

"I was wondering if that's what the third shot was— him finding Baker. But Blake tells me there's been no evidence of another gunfight around the house, and Verrick got back to me awfully quickly..."

Shannon's eyes widened. "There was a third shot?"

"There were three shots, really close together. One was Pierce, obviously, and one was you. But the third sounded an awful lot like Verrick's Army revolver."

Shannon resisted the urge to scoff, but did frown slightly. "Are you sure? You were…distracted."

"I…" Lucas exhaled and looked away. "I don't know. It could've been him confronting Baker, but we never saw the man. I'd kinda hoped… Well, I guess I *wanted* Verrick to have been the one to have shot Pierce, for your sake."

That was unexpected.

"You do? Why? So you don't have to be married to a—"

Her brain caught up with her mouth and snapped it shut before he could hear her bitterness. After all, this was the first time they'd spoken about it, and it would be silly to ruin it.

But he'd heard anyhow, and she watched his expression turn gentle.

"I don't think you're a cold-hearted killer." Still without meeting her eyes, he brought her palm to his lips, the same heart-melting way he'd done before. "I am in awe of the sacrifice you were willing to make for me."

In awe of…?

Shannon swallowed. Those were some of the most beautiful words anyone had ever said to her.

"But I know how you feel about…" *About your father. About Verrick being a killer.*

"I know what I said that afternoon in the kitchen. About not being able to respect a killer. That's what my mother taught me all those years, after all. But *she* was the one who told me to send for Verrick when Baker showed up." His voice dropped to a whisper. "*She* was the one who'd been lying to me all those years."

Shannon could feel his hurt and confusion at his mother's betrayal, but knew there wasn't anything to be done. His mother was gone, unable to explain or defend herself to her only son, and Shannon couldn't do a thing for him, except to maybe comfort him with her presence. Her love.

She reached over and wrapped her other hand around their joined hands, trying to show him without words she understood and would support him in any way she could. He glanced down at their hands, and when he finally looked up, she could swear she saw the beginnings of a wry smile on his lips.

"Verrick told me something that day, Shannon." He held her gaze. "Right after I found out about the baby. He said if you love someone, you'd do *anything* to protect them. When he told me that I thought…well, I thought maybe I understood. I knew I loved you and the baby, and I wondered if maybe that's how he'd felt about me, or about my mother, at one time."

Shannon blinked at her husband, straining to hear him over the blood pounding in her temples. He loved her. To admit it so casually *must* mean it was true. *He loves me.*

Lucas didn't seem aware of her suddenly hopeful heart. "But it wasn't until later that day I knew what he'd said was true." He took a deep breath, one which Shannon felt herself copying. "When I stepped out of that stable and saw Pierce holding a loaded rifle and climbing the steps to get to the house, where I knew *you* were…well… I just…" His grip on her hands tightened. "I knew at that moment I'd do *anything* to protect you, just like Verrick said."

Even become a killer.

Lucas nodded, as if able to understand her thought. "I realize now I was being high-and-mighty, judging Verrick like I did. I realize I'd never really been tested, never had someone I loved so deeply threatened like that. I realize I *would* kill a man to protect someone I loved."

He loved her. He loved her!

But then Lucas looked away. "I'm just…just *so* sorry you had to see me like that."

Shannon blinked, trying to calm her soaring heart long enough to understand what he was saying. "Like what?"

"We were fighting, and when he reached for that gun again, and I knew he could hurt you, I just *snapped*. I didn't just become a killer, I became… Well, Verrick said loving someone meant doing anything to protect them, but what *I* did was horrible. I became a killer with my bare hands."

Shannon shifted slightly and squeezed his hand once, waiting for him to look her way again. When he did, she smiled. "But you didn't, remember?"

"I remember." His chuckle sounded forced, but that was alright, because at least he was trying. "You saved me. I would've *never* asked my wife to pick up a gun, not when I was there to defend her, but you… You did it without asking, and for *my* sake."

"And I'd do it again." She took a deep breath. "Because when you love someone, you'll do *anything* to protect them."

She watched his eyes widen as he understood what she was saying. And then the most beautiful smile spread across his face, tugging at his lips, until his teeth shone bright in the dim light.

"Truly, Shannon? You love me?"

"I've been terrified for weeks, because I didn't think there was any way you could love me as much as I love you."

He untangled his hand from hers and wrapped his good arm around her shoulders. Pulling her against him, he kissed the top of her head. "How could I *not* love you, wife? You're kind and sweet, and make my life wonderful. I love talking with you, and sharing my life with you. And I sure as hell love kissing you."

His lips found her temple, and she smiled.

But her smile faded when she remembered her old fear. "You might not mind being married to a killer—"

He cut her off with a kiss right above her ear. "The fact you were willing to do it for me still leaves me in awe."

She swallowed down the thrill his words gave her, and focused on her other sin. "But being married to a liar is just as bad."

His lips stilled and he straightened. "A liar?"

Shannon kept her eyes glued on the horizon where the pinks were slowly turning to purples.

"I..." She exhaled, then inhaled, as if armoring herself against her own confession. "It's been eating me up inside, the way I lied to you in my letters. Since before I even got here. But then you were so sweet to me, and I thought maybe..." She sighed. "But then you started hiding things, and I knew you were hurt by my lies after all. And meanwhile, I was falling in love—"

"What are you talking about? *What* was I hiding?"

She shrugged. "You weren't telling me everything about Pierce and Baker. Even when I pressed you."

"Oh." In that one syllable, she felt the tension ease out of his shoulder. "Yeah." His arm moved, snuggling her up against him as he shifted his legs out in front of the swing. "I *was* hiding stuff, but I shouldn't have. I was trying to keep you from worrying."

"Keep me from worrying?" She tried to wiggle around in his grip, but no luck. "Knowing you weren't telling me something—such as a gunslinger being hired to kill you!— made me worry more."

Lucas didn't seem bothered by her ire though. Instead, he chuckled. "Yeah, I see that now. I'm real sorry, honey." He smiled that lazy grin of his, and Shannon felt her stomach flip again. "Any woman who is willing to kill a man to protect me, well, she's not the kind of woman I need to worry about worrying. From now on, I'll tell you everything."

"Really?" Her brows went up. "Everything? Even though I lied to you? That must've hurt, for me to show up and you to realize…"

How flawed I am. She couldn't say it.

"Realize *what*, exactly? You didn't lie about how good a cook you are. You didn't lie about your sister—I don't mind having her around, by the way—or about being a pretty good housekeeper. I mean, you can't make soap, but we can keep buying that in town. And you didn't lie about wanting kids"—his fingers trailed down her side, and she shivered—"which has been a definite bonus for me. So what is it you think you lied about?"

Oh God, he was going to make her say it.

"I lied about…" Shannon swallowed and focused on her hands twined in her lap. "I lied about how I look."

"No you didn't." His denial was immediate. "I memorized your letters, Shannon. Blonde hair, blue eyes. That's all you said." He gave the swing a little push. "Now, if you'd said that you were pretty, I would've called you a liar."

Her breath caught on a little sob his casual words surprised out of her.

"See, honey, you're not *just* pretty. You're beautiful. You're graceful. You're the kind of woman I love waking up next to every day."

His words confused her enough to peek up at him to see his smile. "You think I'm beautiful?"

"Tell me about this lie of yours, Shannon."

"My face. It's not beautiful," she confessed. Luckily, he was sitting on her right, so she could turn away. Turn so he couldn't see the birthmark on her left cheek.

"Not—?" Lucas pulled his arm from around her shoulders, and losing that connection almost broke her.

She could feel his gaze on her, hear the confusion in his question. But she couldn't bring herself to point out her flaw.

"Shannon, I don't…" He sighed and ran his hand through his hair. "I don't understand what you're trying to tell me!"

Oh God. He was going to make her say it. She swallowed, and prayed that her voice didn't sound as pitiful as she suspected.

"I'm *not* beautiful, and that's okay. It's the reason I didn't marry in Texas. I wanted *so badly* to get married and have a baby, someone who would love me no matter what I looked like." In her hurry to get her confession out, the words began to trip over one another. "I thought being a mail-order bride would solve that problem; I could marry a man without him seeing me first. But if I'd been honest—honest to you, fair to you I mean—I would've written the truth. I wouldn't have lied—"

"Shannon." His commanding voice cut her off, and he covered her hands—still twisted together on her lap—with his good one. "*What* are you talking about?"

"My face." Why didn't he understand? "I should've been honest about—"

"Your face? What about your face?"

She took a deep breath, closed her eyes, then turned to face him completely. "My birthmark," she whispered.

For a million heartbeats, neither of them moved. Shannon held her breath, waiting for him to speak, waiting for the faintest sound to tell her what he was thinking. When it didn't come, and she'd aged a full year—or so it seemed—she risked a peek through her lashes.

He was smiling. At her.

Surprised, Shannon opened both of her eyes, and his smile grew. His good hand came up and touched her cheek to trace the ugly birthmark, but she forced herself not to flinch.

"How could you *possibly* think this makes you not beautiful?" It wasn't his words so much as his incredulous tone which told her he was telling the truth. "Your beauty isn't just your skin, honey. It's the way your eyes sparkle when you see me in the morning, and the way you smile—you've got this dimple right here—when you think I'm being silly."

He cupped her cheek and drew her face towards his. "It's the way you laugh with me, and the way your eyebrows do this little dippy thing"—he paused to kiss the spot between her eyes—"when you're irritated. You're beautiful because of all of those things put together."

Then he kissed her, and Shannon felt that same heat— the same spark she'd felt when he'd touched her the very first time—spread through her body. She'd missed him these last few days and reveled in the realization he hadn't been avoiding her at all. Unabashedly, she threw her arms around his neck and kissed him back.

And when they both emerged for air, a lifetime later, she was smiling.

"Yeah, honey," Lucas drawled, "like that."

And then he kissed her birthmark.

Shannon shuddered at the feel of his lips against her skin, kissing the part of her she'd been so ashamed of for so long. The part that, despite all of her fears, he really didn't seem to mind.

"You don't mind people will stare at your wife?"

"Mmmm." He was kissing her earlobe now. "They'd be fools not to stare."

"I mean in pity." She was trying to focus, but his lips

made it difficult. "My whole life, people have stared at me in pity. *That's* why I'm sorry I didn't tell you…"

Lucas straightened, but not so far her arms would fall away from his shoulders. "If a person can't see past one little birthmark to see the beauty of your smile or eyes or heart, then they *are* fools. *You are beautiful*, Shannon Montgomery Ryan, and if it takes the rest of our lives to prove it to you, well…" He smiled that smile she loved so much. "Then I'll look forward to the challenge."

And just like that, everything was right and good in her world.

Shannon couldn't help the noise she made—something between a whimper and a squeal—when she tightened her hold on him and pressed herself against his chest. "That's the most wonderful thing anyone has ever said to me, husband!"

"Oh yeah?" Lucas shifted, so his good arm was around her once more. "How about this? I love you, wife. I'm going to love you for all of our days."

She kissed his jaw. "And I love you, Lucas. I've never known a man like you, so caring and optimistic. Thank you for showing me the blessings in life.

"Blessings? Like what?"

She smiled. "Like the baby we created together. You're going to be the most wonderful father."

When he stiffened, Shannon immediately knew why, and she unlaced one hand to press her palm against his cheek. "You really are, Lucas. You're going to be a wonderful father, no matter what role Verrick plays in our lives. Your mother's teachings will ensure you won't turn out like Thomas Ryan, and your own sense of honor has done the rest. You're going to be a wonderful Daddy."

If she hadn't been looking directly into those beautiful

golden-brown eyes, she would've missed the tears gathered in them.

"You really think so?"

She kissed him lightly. "I *know* so. You already love this baby more than anything else, so how could I be wrong?"

He stood up so suddenly she squealed in surprise when she was yanked up too. "You're wrong, Mrs. Ryan." Smiling down at her in the dusk, he looked far too handsome for his own good. "I love *you* more than anything else, and I mean to start proving it to you right now."

Knowing what he had in mind, Shannon beamed. "I might take some convincing, husband, but I look forward to your efforts." She was careful not to jostle his arm when she pressed against him. "I love you, Lucas."

"And I love you, wife."

And as he lowered his lips to hers for another gentle, warm kiss, Shannon knew the truth. They each had their own troubles—she'd never be conventionally beautiful, and he would have to learn to forgive his mother—but they also had each other. And truly, in this world, that's all that mattered.

Loving one another.

Epilogue

"So then the sailor says; 'That's not an oar, that's me sister!'" Cora deadpanned as she lifted a wet plate from the wash basin.

Even expecting the bawdy punchline, Lucas burst into surprised laughter as he took the plate and began drying.

"Have you been trading jokes with Lefty?" His chuckles subsided as he put the plate in the cabinet. "I swear that sounds like something he would say."

"I never give away my sources," his sister-in-law said with a wink. She turned back to the dishes, but threw her words over her shoulder towards him. "But you have some explaining to do, mister."

"Me?" What had he done wrong?

Cora's chin jerked towards the table. "Shannon isn't laughing, which means she didn't get it, which means *you* haven't done a good enough job teaching her how to be naughty."

From behind them, at the kitchen table, his wife snorted tiredly. "I understood the joke, Cora, I just didn't think it was worth laughing at. *Some* of us have standards, you know."

Lucas leaned around Cora, even as he dried another plate, to smile at Shannon. "And *some* of us love you for your standards."

"*Some* of us were hoping our sister would start making bawdy jokes *too*!"

"I'm not bawdy," quipped Shannon. "I'm pregnant."

Cora burst into laughter and Lucas joined. Even Shannon, looked utterly exhausted, chuckled. The last few weeks had been rough on her, but Doc Vickers in town insisted it was normal to be so tired in the early months of a pregnancy and assured Shannon she'd have more energy by the end of summer.

For her sake, Lucas hoped so. Still, he had to admit he found joy in heading upstairs right after dinner and holding her until she fell asleep. Sometimes he'd fall asleep too, and sometimes he'd get up and go back downstairs to sit at his mother's small desk to work. But either way, it was nice to hold her as she slipped into dreamland.

On the nights he went back downstairs to the kitchen, he'd occasionally run into Cora, coming in from a twilight walk around the ranch. He worried about her, especially with no sign of what happened to Baker, but she assured him she was safe. She also flat-out refused to tell him what she was doing, saying only "an artist needs inspiration," so he quit bugging her about it.

Now, he grinned fondly at his wife. "Dinner was delicious, honey." Still holding the damp dish towel, he slid into the chair next to her and threw one arm across its back. "I wish you wouldn't work so hard, but it *was* good."

Her smile was as lovely as always. "I knew you loved my fried chicken. I wanted to make your birthday special."

"How could it not be?" He tugged her shoulder closer

until her head tilted towards him, and he placed a chaste kiss on her lips. "I have the best present a man could ask for."

From across the kitchen, Cora interrupted. "A sister-in-law with impeccable comedic timing?"

Lucas didn't tear his gaze away from Shannon's beautiful blue eyes when he called out, "Not even close." He lowered his voice when he said to his wife, "I have a wife who loves me despite my faults and a baby on the way."

Shannon's small hand came up to cup his cheek. "I do love you, Lucas. And no matter how annoying she is, Cora loves you too."

He smiled. "Then I'm a lucky man to be surrounded by my family."

"Well, since you two are just going to keep ignoring me, I'll eat this birthday cake by myself." Cora moved to the other side of the table and carefully set down a platter with the most beautiful lemon cake on it.

Lucas stared at the cake for a long moment, before glancing back at Shannon. "You did that?" His gaze was drawn inexorably to the dessert. "You made that for me?"

"Happy birthday, husband."

He couldn't help the smile that bloomed. "I don't think I've ever seen such a pretty cake!" He'd always had a soft spot for sweets, but his mother hadn't been a baker. "In fact, I think it might be my first ever birthday cake."

"Then I'm glad I could make it for you."

"And I'm glad I could help by standing around and watch— Oh!" Cora's quip was cut off by a gasp.

When Lucas managed to tear his gaze away from the delectable-looking cake, he saw his sister-in-law staring at the doorway. Not sure what to expect, Lucas tightened his hold on Shannon's shoulder and turned in his chair.

And slowly rose to his feet when he saw Verrick

standing there in the doorway looking, for the first time Lucas could remember…*hesitant*. Unsure.

The other man's golden gaze locked on Cora's, but after a moment, his attention shifted back to Lucas. He nodded once, still looking as if he wasn't quite certain of his welcome.

Lucas wasn't sure what to say. He'd invited Verrick to dinner a few weeks ago, and the older man had been surprised, judging from his expression. He'd hesitated, then shaken his head in almost an apology, which made Lucas wonder what was keeping Verrick away. Did he *want* to spend time with them? Was something holding him apart?

That had been during the same confrontation when Lucas had asked about his mother. He hadn't had the guts to come right out and ask Verrick how he'd managed to father him, but the older man had understood.

After a long silence, during which Verrick seemed to struggle to find words, he'd finally said: "I have never forced myself on a woman."

And that was that.

Verrick hadn't seemed interested in saying more, and Lucas had been supremely uncomfortable with the discussion, so they'd both dropped it.

Maybe one day he'd find answers from this man who was his father, but maybe not. Maybe there were secrets Verrick was keeping for a reason, secrets that could change Lucas's memory of his mother. He wasn't sure, but he'd realized something surprising; He trusted Verrick. He trusted the man to protect him and his family, and he trusted that on some level, Verrick cared for *him*.

And on some level, he cared for the older man too.

He was the first to break the silence. "Would you like some cake?"

Verrick's eerie golden eyes flicked to the table and to

Cora once more, and he seemed to consider it. Finally, he nodded again. "I am partial to sweets."

"My mother certainly wasn't." Had Lucas inherited this from his father, the man standing before him?

Verrick's eyebrow twitched. "Not that I can recall."

And Lucas smiled slightly to realize he was sharing reminiscences about his mother with the man who'd fathered him. They weren't the type of memories he would've preferred, but still… There was a strange sort of *rightness* to the whole encounter.

Verrick stepped further into the room. "Today is your birthday."

He'd remembered.

From the table, Shannon spoke up. "It's traditional to wish someone a happy birthday, you know."

"And will my words change the state of his birthday? Will my saying so make it a happier day for him?"

It sounded as if the two of them had had this conversation before.

There was a grin in Shannon's voice when she said, "Yes, Verrick. I really think it would."

Lucas turned slightly to see his wife staring at his father with a sort of challenge on her face and a smile on her lovely lips. And Verrick seemed to understand.

He inclined his head to Shannon, then turned his attention once more to Lucas. "Happy birthday, Lucas."

Inexplicably, Shannon was right. Verrick's words *did* make Lucas's day happier.

"Thank you." He gestured to the seat beside Cora's. "Would you like to join us?"

Verrick stared at him a few moments longer than comfortable, then turned his attention to Cora. Another pause, then he nodded. "Yes. Very much."

Cora smiled. "You're just saying that because you want to try this cake Shannon made."

The older man didn't blink, didn't react. His eyes flicked to Lucas. "Possibly."

From the table, Shannon mock-whispered to her sister, "I think that was supposed to be a joke. We're still working on the concept."

"I think you should work with him on delivery," Cora whispered back, grinning at Verrick the entire time.

"He doesn't have your superb sense of comedic timing, obviously."

"*Obviously*," Cora responded. "I'll have to teach him the one about the man and the horse."

"Just leave out the hand gestures, please."

Lucas could barely contain his laughter as he watched his father—the west's most notorious gunslinger—glance helplessly between the two women, obviously not understanding their teasing.

Here Lucas was, standing in his kitchen, surrounded by his family on his birthday. He had a wife whom he adored, a baby on the way, and a sister-in-law who kept life interesting. He had a ranch he could build into a success, a delicious-looking lemon cake, and friends who cared about him. And now, thanks to a twist of fate, he had the chance to get to know his real father.

When he clapped Verrick on the shoulder, the man looked startled at the casual familiarity. That didn't stop Lucas from smiling into golden eyes a few shades lighter than his own, and jerking his thumb to the table—and the delicious cake.

"If you want dessert, you have to put up with these two."

"I've endured worse." Verrick's delivery would've been deadpan, if he had any other tone to compare it to.

Shannon mock-whispered, "His jokes are getting better."

"Almost as good as mine," Cora responded.

Lucas's grin grew as he watched Verrick's brow raise.

"Welcome to the family, Father."

More Sunset Valley Books

Ahhh! Caroline! You can't just leave us with such a tantalizing hint there *might* be something going on between Verrick and Cora, then end the book! *Ahhhhh*!

Don't worry, my friends! Honestly, Verrick's romance was the one *I've* been looking forward to reading as well...so here it is! *Verrick's Vixen* is waiting! Have I mentioned how much I love Verrick?

And when you're done with Verrick and Cora, you can pick up *Abigail's Adventure*, the story of Matthias Blake's—the foreman at Sunset Valley —romance.

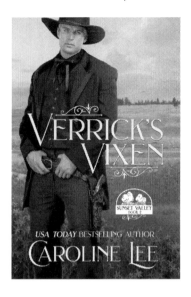

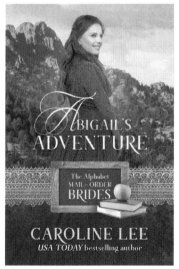

If you've enjoyed Shannon and Lucas's romance, I urge you to friend me on Facebook or follow me on Twitter. I

frequently post fun stories, links to great books, and cute animal pictures.
If you'd like to keep up with my books, read deleted scenes, or receive exclusive free books, sign up for my newsletter.

———

And if newsletters aren't your thing, come join my reader group, Caroline's Cohort!

———

Please consider leaving a review—it's bread and butter to an author like me. It's proven that books with more reviews —and they don't have to be effusive—sell better, and I appreciate each and every one. *Thank you!*

Acknowledgments

As always, a big thank you to Alyssa and Merry Farmer, to my beta readers and Cohort members, and to my editor CM Wright.

About the Author

Caroline Lee has been reading romance for so long that her fourth-grade teacher used to make her cover her books with paper jackets. But it wasn't until she (mostly) grew up that she realized she could *write* it too. So she did.

Caroline is living her own little Happily Ever After in NC with her husband, sons, and brand-new daughter, Princess Wiggles. And while she doesn't so much "suffer" from Pittakionophobia as think that all you people who enjoy touching Band-Aids and stickers are the real weirdos, she *does* adore rodents, and never met a wine she didn't like. Caroline was named Time Magazine's Person of the Year in 2006 and is really quite funny in person. Promise.

You can find her at www.CarolineLeeRomance.com.

facebook.com/carolineleeauthor
instagram.com/authorcarolinelee
bookbub.com/authors/caroline-lee-c918b5ae-ab71-437d-98f1-5a2b09b055f3

Sunset Valley

(Black Aces prequel)

Lucas's Lady

Verrick's Vixen

Abigail's Adventure

Black Aces

Ante Up

Three of a Kind

Wild Card

Everland Ever After:

A fairy-tale town set in the wilds of the old west!

Little Red (free on all retailers)

Ella

Beauty

The Stepmother

Rapunzelle

Briar Rose

Rose Red

The Mermaid

The Prince's Pea

The Sweet Cheyenne Quartet:

Love for all seasons in nineteenth-century Wyoming.

A Cheyenne Christmas

A Cheyenne Celebration

A Cheyenne Thanksgiving

A Cheyenne Christmas Homecoming

The Mothers of Sweet Cheyenne

Where They Belong

Sign up for Caroline's Newsletter to receive exclusive content and freebies, as well as first dibs on her books! Or if newsletters aren't your thing, follow her on Bookbub for a quick, concise new release alert every time she publishes a book!

Made in the USA
Las Vegas, NV
03 August 2023